The Falls of the Wyona

The Falls of the Wyona

a novel

❧

DAVID BRENDAN HOPES

🐾 Red Hen Press | *Pasadena, CA*

Book layout by Mark E. Cull

ISBN-13: 9781597098939

The National Endowment for the Arts, the Los Angeles County Arts Commission, the Ahmanson Foundation, the Dwight Stuart Youth Fund, the Max Factor Family Foundation, the Pasadena Tournament of Roses Foundation, the Pasadena Arts & Culture Commission and the City of Pasadena Cultural Affairs Division, the City of Los Angeles Department of Cultural Affairs, the Audrey & Sydney Irmas Charitable Foundation, the Kinder Morgan Foundation, the Meta & George Rosenberg Foundation, the Allergan Foundation, and the Riordan Foundation partially support Red Hen Press.

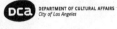

ART WORKS.
arts.gov

Enriching Lives
Los Angeles County Arts Commission

DEPARTMENT OF CULTURAL AFFAIRS
City of Los Angeles

First Edition
Published by Red Hen Press
www.redhen.org

For
Ruth and Harris Summers

The Falls of the Wyona

I

Rain came quick and sharp. It dimpled the river and made it flash where it had been the flat gray color of the clouds. You had to stop and think what it reminded you of. Then the rain stopped and the clouds broke and everything above the river stood mirrored in perfect detail in the river's face. Except there, right where we were. Water dripped from a branch high above us, and when the drops hit the pool river, the picture scattered and blurred. When the pool calmed, you could see our two shapes, my round buzzed head, his long movie-star hair lifting and settling back in the breeze. We were standing the same way and looking in the same place. You look in the shadows to get past the glare on the water to see fish and crayfish and the like, but I wasn't looking at that. I was looking at him. I'd just used the phrase "best friend" a moment before in my heart, though I was afraid to say it out loud. Vince was funny about things sometimes. There were so many ways he could take it wrong.

Forty feet farther down, the river spread out into a fan. Then it disappeared. You know it was going over the falls, the brown Wyona flashing suddenly white and gold in its hundred foot drop to the white stones, but it sure looked like it just disappeared. The rising cloud of mist is the Wyona saying goodbye. We were wary of going too much closer. Rumor suggested eddies and undertows that would shoot you over the falls as soon as look at you. Plenty of kids had vanished that way. People in town kept lists, and though the lists differed from one another, their cautionary effect was undeniable. "The Falls claims one each generation," people said. People say a lot of things.

Tilden's uncle was one the Falls claimed. If you go into their house there's a picture of Tilden's uncle—his mom's brother or something—with dry yellow willow twisted around the picture frame. He looks like every other kid in the world, though with the funny clothes they had back then. I thought it was odd for him to be dead and all of us alive.

Tilden thrashed around over in the weeds pursuing something. A little nervous close to the brink, he did his fishing from the shore, poking through the arrowhead and cattails for anything that moved. He'd learned to cuss in an abstract, uncommitted way, so we heard him over there saying, in a normal tone of voice, almost politely, "bastard" and "son of a bitch" when something eluded his grasp. It was froggy in the pools for being so high up and so close to the falls. I guess the frogs came down from the hills, like the river did, except they knew when to stop.

Vince kept standing up and looking over his shoulder into the woods.

I knew what Vince would do. I knew how he would do it. We were one person, sometimes. There were photos of us playing under the sweet gum in Grandpa's yard, the two of us in diapers and the leaves of the sweet gum like stars behind our heads. I must have known Mom and Dad and Grandpa and all them first, but I don't remember anyone before Vince. Dark hair. Dark eyes, dark soul. Different from me. They put us together so we could have a friend from the first, and it worked.

Now he was looking over his shoulder in that way he had.

"He'll come," I said, though I wasn't sure whether he'd come or not. We were waiting for Glen. I wasn't sure whether I wanted Glen to come or not.

Two big hawks kept house in a pine overhanging the river then. The lady was out hunting. The gentleman stood at the edge of their nest screaming at us not to come any closer. We had no intention of coming closer.

I kept wondering if I would remember that moment, or any like it. Speaking of it now, forty years later, answers the question.

Vince took to Glen the minute he moved to town from St. Louis. I didn't have time for him. He was citified or sissified or something I couldn't put my finger on. A boy with a comb in his pocket, and with the willingness to use it in public, was an oddity in our neck of the woods. Glen would have had a bad first day at school, except Vince left the gaggle of boys he was the center of and walked to where the new kid was standing alone on the playground. This was not the usual way Vince worked. He liked being the center. He liked mocking those who weren't at the center. In being peripheral, they were culpable of something, even if it was hard to say what. This time, it was different. I examined Glen to discover why the different treatment, but I couldn't see it. Glen was as different from Tilden and me as a kid could get, so maybe Vince wanted to fill in whatever it was he missed in us. It was hard showing up in the middle of the school year, but that wasn't our fault. Snow peppered the ground and everyone had to wear the stupid hats they'd gotten for Christmas. Vince walked over in his stupid hat and stood by Glen in his stupid hat, and pretty soon all of us in our stupid hats toddled over to bask in Vince's radiance.

Glen's presence there was incidental to everyone but Vince. He was in, Glen was, by accident of proximity.

Glen became one of us. That was OK, because most of the town gangs had at least four and there were things we couldn't accomplish with just the three of us that had been. I liked Glen before long. He was smart, and certain things you could talk about with him that you couldn't with others. You could hear longhair music from the station in Charlottesville sometimes, and he could tell you what it was and why it sounded like that. Tilden liked everybody, or didn't mention it if he didn't, so that was not a problem.

Vince brought Tilden into my life. It was winter, and I'd been scolded for something—I couldn't have learned much of a lesson if I didn't even remember what it was—and I'd been staring out the window for a while feeling sorry for myself. Hearing my big brother two rooms away talking in that man's voice he always had didn't help. I would never grow up. I would never be like Andy, never be the boy my parents apparently wanted me to be. They always said, "Be yourself," but that was clearly not what they actually wanted. I stared into the darkening gray light. After a while I saw shapes materialize far down the street, where it curved away into a sweep of familiar hills. They were the same hills I'd always known, but in my misery they might have been the Caucasus. The two moving shapes seemed small in the vastness of the coming storm. They made me think of the Magi on the Christmas cards, processing through the moonlit wilderness, from where one knew not, toward what one could only suppose. They moved slowly, steadily, getting bigger as they came. When they moved close enough, I saw two boys, one in a snowsuit, one in a heavy green army jacket with a floppy hat pulled tight over his ears. As their feet touched the edge of our drive, snow began to descend, carefully and beautifully, everywhere. I waved. They waited while I got my snowsuit and boots on. Of course they were Vince and Tilden. They must have walked a long, long way. They had pulled on their snow suits and ugly caps to come to me in the teeth of the blizzard.

The new boy said, "Tilden."

I said, "Arden."

Vince and Tilden filled the time waiting for me to don my snowsuit by sticking their tongues out into the falling snow to catch the flakes. Coming through the door I stuck my tongue out too, automatically, before a word had passed between us. Tilden said, "They're different flavors, you know, depending on whether it's before or after Christmas." I never doubted it.

"Vince-and-Tilden" would be one name to me forever after. To the rest of the town we were "those three."

I thought our community closed then, but it didn't. We met Glen, too, in winter, and though the snowsuits vanished, the absurd hats did not. Our shadows on the snow made us look like Mongol horsemen in vast headdresses. I would have voted no on him but there was no vote, and afterwards I was glad, for Glen brought something new to the group. I couldn't say what, except that adults seemed to like him and that might come in handy. Glen was older than the rest of us without actually *being* older, if you know what I mean. He was finished. Just like Tilden would be finished perfect when he reached fifteen, and never after in his life be older than fifteen. Me? I have no idea. You have to ask somebody else.

Glen had never been to the Falls. We discovered it ourselves the summer before he came, but kept it secret. All the neighborhood gangs thought they had discovered it themselves and nobody else knew. The Falls of the Wyona were sacred. Set apart. So it had been for generations of boys since the town was settled, and probably before that for the Indian boys. I wasn't sure of inviting a boy who'd just moved to town. A boy didn't go to the Falls just because he wanted to. He might stumble upon it himself, in which case destiny gave him a kind of celebrity, or he might be invited by those who'd been there before. That was the usual way.

Glen wasn't woodsy, so the likelihood of his finding it himself was slight. We had to give him the Falls or he would have done without. It was up to him to give us something back. We waited to find out what.

I'd found the Falls for us. That will be a matter of pride for me until the end of days. It happened as I was leaving my piano lesson with Miss Phoebe. I didn't like piano that much, but I liked Miss Phoebe, a high school girl who gave lessons for a while until she could go off to the conservatory after graduation. The high school had a conservatory, but it was full of plants and botany experiments and it was a while before I could figure out what that had to do with piano. Anyway, I was standing on her porch with my hand in her hand. She was giving me final instructions for the week, holding my fingers in the arch she wanted to see over the keys next time. That's what she thought she was doing, but I thought she was holding my hand, and the thrill going through me was difficult to understand, much less to express. When I pondered it afterward, I wondered if her intentions were as pure as they seemed, or if maybe she was flirting just a little bit. Anyway, I cast my eyes away so I wouldn't have to look at her as well as have my hand in hers on the front porch, when I saw, way off, a cloud that looked like a tornado in the pure yellow evening sky.

"What's that?" I said. I had to pull my hand away to point, and so the moment came to an end.

"You never saw that before?" Miss Phoebe said. "Something about the river. About the Falls. It happens almost every night, as far as I can tell. This is a good place to watch it from."

I swear I had never heard the word "Falls" associated with the Wyona before that minute. Little tiny falls punctuated the length of it flowing through town, but nothing to raise a cloud like the one I saw. Two days later was Saturday. I packed myself a lunch and headed out toward the twisty cloud. I started right at Miss Phoebe's porch, where I'd seen it, and where she could see me, and maybe admire my adventurous spirit. We knew the encircling woods pretty well, and when the paths I knew came to an end, I felt confident to take the new, strange ones, dead reckoning the ones that led to the river. I'd almost never gone anywhere without Vince, or without Vince and Tilden together.

Roaring told me when I neared the river. The Wyona made a sound flowing through town, of course, rippling past the bridges and the stands of green reeds, but nothing like this: thunderous, deep, cataclysmic. If I hadn't had the classroom maps to tell me different, I would have thought I found the edge of the world, where the oceans pour into the void.

When I came into the clearing I'd wished I'd brought Vince and Tilden, for it was too big for me alone. The forest opened on a keyhole of blue sky—that lustrous sad china blue that leans toward evening—with the Wyona flashing at the bottom of it. The river ran through trees and grasses in town, but here it ran over pale yellow stone and, at the western edge of the clearing, disappeared. The roaring came from the point of disappearance, as did a cloud of mist sometimes hesitant among the rocks, sometimes billowing over and back into the river's face. I didn't need to go there right away. I knew it was the Falls. No one ever spoke of it. It couldn't have opened over night, but maybe it did, and mine were the first mortal eyes ever to take it in. I entertained that thought.

I was a kid, but I wasn't that dumb. I knew the Falls must be a secret kept by the adults for reasons at the moment past telling. The cloud blowing back from the rocks under the Falls was formidable, but not dark like the cloud I saw from Miss Phoebe's porch, and lacked its own twisting life. Maybe a trick of evening light? I didn't know. But that day I'd seen enough. I needed to scurry if I were going to get home before dark. The paths past a certain point were unfamiliar and I was, after all, very small under those looming trees.

Vince flat out didn't believe me until I took him and Tilden there the next Saturday. He was used to being the big man, the pioneer. He nearly always got there first, wherever we were going, whatever new skill we were trying to master. I decided not to gloat over this, our single greatest discovery, all mine. On that second trip, Tilden and Vince and I, we discovered the mystery of the cloud.

Glen likely didn't know he was being tested, but he was. Glen was tall, frail-looking, pale, with hair that was nearly white then but would darken some before high school. His gray eyes were a plus. A lot of heroes had gray eyes. Writers are very specific about that. They made him a possibility, the eyes did, though the rest of him, his frailness, his trace of sissy, made it seem unlikely at first that his companion-ship would be rewarding. We told him how to get to the Falls, giving the precise instructions only boys know how to give. We told him when. We told him everyone had to go alone the first time. This was a lie, but I insisted. I suppose it was my subtle way of emphasizing that I had first gone there alone and had some right to make the rules. The rest was up to him.

I assumed he'd get lost and have to be brought out by us at a later time, but there he was, not too long after Vince had started anxiously to look for him.

"Glen," Vince said under his breath.

"It's a long way," Glen said when he came into in range, pushing out of the scrub trees at the edge of the stone. Tilden said, "Hell," appreciatively.

Vince held out his hand to steady Glen across a gap.

"Not that long. You get used to it."

"Your directions were pretty good."

Tilden slipped into the river and said, "Son of a bitch." Since his shoes were wet anyway, he stayed in the water, looking for a shallow place to ford over to us.

A dragonfly buzzed the top of Glen's shoes. The dragonfly was so blue it made the sky look green. Glen watched while the bug lit on his boot toe and then zoomed away. I could see Vince's face taking on the same expression as mine. Glen stood for a moment, looking around, taking everything in. One had to do that his first time at the Falls, just look and look. He put his hands on his waist and turned slowly, like a lighthouse that had to cover the whole sea.

"Damn," he said, "The river just disappears."

"Yeah it does," Tilden called from the midst of the river. He was making a face because the water had something brown and slimy on the bottom of it. "Go on and look."

Glen moved along the bank some, rolled his cuffs up, then dropped into the water, quieter and smoother than Tilden. It was August and the river ran very low. The water looked more transparent when something was in it—the brown bottom made it look like it was brown all through—and a boy's white legs shone golden underneath. You had to go slower as the water deepened. Glen went ceremonially slow. The dragonfly followed him to the middle of the stream, glancing off his shoulder, wheeling away, circling back again. We hadn't warned him of the eddies and undertows, but somehow he eluded them and came to the very lip of the precipice.

"The brown slimy stuff is really slick," Tilden said. Glen nodded.

He stood there at the brink a long time, looking. Still, he couldn't have taken it all in. This was the great gorge of the Wyona. The river writhed under him like a wounded dragon. Two states moved out from the gorge in green wilderness and white mountain rock. Far off there was a glitter of sun glancing off a moving car, in the remoteness where there were roads and cars and people other than ourselves.

Glen looked a long time before he moved again. Two steps the wrong way would have sent him over the falls. He didn't move his feet, but put his hands on his knees and began to bend in tiny increments, easing ever more of his weight over the brink. He looked like a diver readying for the dive. He balanced on the very edge. He did a handstand, feet in the air, hands on the slick brown rock at the very lip of the Falls. The three of us recognized the motion from gym class, from Mr. Lecheck's everlasting obsession with tumbling and gymnastics. Glen did a handstand on a slippery boulder, one side of which was probable and the other side certain death. Up he went. It looked effortless. I always had to kick a little. He hit the handstand and just hovered there like it was nothing at all. He looked like an odd little Atlas, holding up the sky with his feet.

Vince tensed beside me. I heard him say in a tiny voice, "Glen—"

Glen understood without being told (and that's the way it had to happen) that some high deed was necessary for full acceptance of an outlander to the Order of the Falls. None of us had thought of a handstand. I liked this kid better and better. Glen hung suspended between the river and the empty air. The dragonfly landing on his shoulder could send him down. Then he just stopped. He folded down and stood on his feet again. The stream ran almost uninterrupted for a wide space as it leapt over the cliff, but a few big rocks studded the edge of it. Glen made for one of these. He leapt from one to the other. He maneuvered himself around to find accommodation in the current, and he sat down.

Vince dropped with a loud splash into the river. The weight of the water hindered his effort to run, so he looked a little stupid thrashing through it with his elbows up. Tilden and I laughed before we realized how serious he was. He got to Glen, reached out and pulled him by his shirt. He said, "Enough."

Glen smiled a big smile. He knew whatever the game was, he had won. He was in. We were the best gang in town, and he was in.

Vince's face was white, the skin under his sideburns pouring sweat. He waded back without Glen like something in the river embarrassed him.

Glen and Tilden stayed out in the middle of the river talking. Once Tilden got in he didn't want to get out. They were out there talking, play-pushing one another to see if they could get the other to fall into the stream. They were laughing like little boys. I suppose that's what we were, but the Falls made you feel different. Vince came up close to me, the way he did when he wanted to tell something that was just between us.

"Arden?"

"Yeah?"

"I feel funny."

"What do you mean funny? You sick?"

"I don't know. It feels—funny."

"What? Your stomach?"

"I guess so."

"Vertigo, maybe, you were so close to the edge—"

I wasn't a doctor, so I waited a minute to see if he had anything else to say, then I said, "He did great."

"Who did?"

"Glen."

"Yeah."

Vince was holding his stomach, but I didn't really think that's what hurt him. The boy had slammed down a whole bottle of cherry pop on the way up and belched out the gas in a magnificent elk-bellow just before we hit the river. I didn't think there was anything wrong with his stomach.

Then he said, "I felt . . . something . . ."

"What?"

"I've never been afraid before. Not like that."

"Afraid of what?"

"If Glen . . ."

Vince was shaking a little. I pushed up hard against him so he'd have my warmth to calm him. I didn't want to say what I was thinking, which was "good." Vince could be a little harsh. He could put a distance between himself and the weakness of others. Cold, he was, sometimes. It hurt Tilden more than it did me. It hurt kids who weren't one of us, because they didn't know it was just normal and he wasn't mad at them. It was good if concern for someone made him sick this one time.

"Anyway, he made it."

I agreed, "Yes he did. Flying colors, I'd say."

Vince would bunch up a fist and hold the fist against your rib cage when he was talking seriously about something. I don't think he knew he did it. The touch was so light that you didn't always know it was happening. Vince was worked up this time, and I could feel the fist there, warm and urgent. I never moved away. As long as the fist was there, it meant the issue had not been settled.

"Glen—" he said.

"Glen what?"

He might have said it. He might have said it right then and been done with it, but I felt his fist drop away from my side. Vince looked away from me and I looked where he was looking. It was too bright where Glen sat. I had to look away.

Changing my glance upstream, pondering all these things in my heart, I saw movement in the river that did not look like the river. The light made the water gold-brown, and the thing in the river was gold-brown, so it took a moment before I saw a dog, a golden Lab, struggling in the current. I was already moving toward the lip of the pool when I started shouting, "Glen! Tilden!"

The dog was a good swimmer, but the current was too fast, the rocks too slippery. She would muscle herself to the side and try to climb the bank, but her foothold would betray her and back she'd splash into the river. I was thinking if only she had hands, already aware beneath the panic that the hands she needed were mine. I hit the river's edge. I jumped. *Whack* I went on the wet stone. A blaze of shock went up my ankles and was gone. I was all right. The dog came on at an amazing rate. You could see in her eyes that she had run out of ideas . . . except me . . . she saw me and began paddling wildly, clawing the slick rocks underneath when she could, trying to get to the spot where I could grab her. I knelt and reached my hands out over the river. I got as deep in as I dared, what with the red goo on the rocks like oil and the weight of the river pouring over the lip murderous and irresistible. I leaned over as far as I could. If she was heavier than I thought, I'd be plunging with her into the emerald gorge. *Whack!* I felt her. I grabbed. The dog relaxed into my arms, but I wasn't strong enough to pull her out. She whimpered and licked my face, as if saying, "I know this isn't going to work, but thanks for trying."

I decided it was going to work. I slipped a few inches farther, but dug in my heels. I hooked my hands behind her front legs, pulling hard. She was not coming out of the water, but neither was she going over the Falls. I didn't know how long I could hold on, or when I'd get another idea. Then Tilden came beside me, pulling on the poor dog too. I shifted my grip so he pulled her right leg and I her left. The three of us were enough. The Lab came out of the water and onto the white shingle, on top of us as we fell flat upon our backs. Glen cheered wildly from the wall. The dog was trying to lick our faces off.

The Lab was generous with her thank yous, but she had a life which she needed to take up again, just like everybody else. At last she waggled her way back into the forest, heading for town, stopping every now and then to look over her shoulder and bark one more thanks. We watched her go.

Tilden said, "You know, it could be that we were brought here at this day and hour so we could fetch that puppy from the river."

Glen said, "It's also possible that the pup was sent to us. A test, you know. She had the look about her. Like she was in control the whole time, waiting to see what we would do."

Vinny said nothing. It wasn't like him.

The sun moved and the glancing of it off the Falls changed to glory. You had to hold your hand in front of your eyes, or look away. From the air or from some point downstream it must have seemed a snow-white conflagration. Gulls from saltwater far away lived at the Falls, circling white upon white all day so far as we could tell. We threw shadows to the east as tall as trees. We sat and ate sandwiches and cookies in a cup of fire.

High in the north a cloud formed, fast, dark, undulating in a way unlike the wind. I elbowed Vinny and he looked. Tilden saw what we saw and pulled himself up on the bank to be standing on solid ground for it. Glen, oblivious at first, noticed all eyes on a certain spot in the sky. He turned his gaze there.

"What the—?"

It was the greatest thing that happened around our town—twice a day at that, once coming and once going. People talked about it sometimes, but many had never seen it. Some people don't see anything at all. The cloud grew, darkened, and tilted toward us at about twice the velocity of the wind. It did not come direct, but detoured and looped and undulated, as though there were obstacles in the clear air we couldn't see.

"What the—" Glen tried again, pulling himself up off his cozy place on the rocks as Tilden had done.

Vinny stopped chewing on the bit of grass he'd stuck into his mouth. I could see him looking up into the air like a contemplative calf, cud suspended. Something changed. Light thickened. The air condensed. Wind came up and began to make noise in the angles of the rocks and in the distant trees. Shapes appeared in the purpling vault of the sky, at first a few, then more, and then more. They approached, their dark mass hovering upon uncountable wings. Whatever one might have imagined, they were birds. As the first outriders circled high up in the air, they were joined by others, ten and then hundreds and then of thousands of others. Were there a million? We stopped counting or estimating. Except for far away, at the horizon, they filled the sky. The noise they made was as loud as the falls, though higher pitched and more varied. We were caught between two parts of a tremendous music. Glen covered his ears.

Black ribbons of birds joined and separated and interwove. It was more intricate than it appeared at distance, less a funnel than a great folded cloth weaving and raveling. What was remarkable close up was that there were no collisions, no tragedies midair, but a dance which never went wrong and never varied in grace. The black shapes darted and twittered. They began to whirl above the gorge like water in a draining tub.

"Birds," Tilden said, unnecessarily. "A million billion birds. There's a cave under the falls—I guess there is; nobody's ever been there—and they sleep there at night and fly out through a hole in the water in the morning, and come back at night."

Vince said, "They're blackbirds."

Glen corrected, "They're swifts."

The swifts circled for a while. Something boiled up from the gorge to meet them. We looked down and saw bats—hundreds, perhaps, but nowhere near the myriad myriads of birds in the air above us. Bats zoomed out of the falls as the swifts zoomed in, one battalion replacing another in the seething air. The bats did not go straight up into the whirling mass, but spread out into the gorge, low and cautious. A few flapped directly over our heads, so you could see the little smiles on their faces, the thin squeaking which is what a human can hear of their song. The swifts let the bats clear, then the whole mass of them leapt up a hundred feet higher into the air, like a diver bouncing on the board before descent. It was plain that one bird flew at the head, one bird leading them. Whether it was the same bird all the time or a new one each night, one didn't know. When this vanguard bird judged everything felt right, down he fell, power-diving directly into the plunging face of the falls.

Twenty by twenty they entered the gap in the waters. We thought they could never be done at that rate, but they could. We watched until they were safe in, except for stragglers which kept arriving, one by one, two by two. Loners would be homing most of the night. We allowed our concentration to lapse, so we could talk of what we saw.

Tilden said, "Swifts. Is that really their name, or is that just how they are?"

"Both," Glen answered.

Tilden peered steadily down into the purple gorge. He said, "If you wanted to kill yourself, that would be the way to do it."

I offered that it wouldn't be like killing yourself at all, but a sort of sacrament. Diving into the middle of the world.

It was getting ever darker and we couldn't see it very well, but Tilden's voice said, "People do it all the time."

"Do what?"

"Throw themselves over the Falls."

"How do you know?"

"Stands to reason. My uncle did. I think that's what happened. It's there. The Falls and the gorge. It's big, and nobody told us about it. They're protecting us. Must be some sort of temptation. Must be people sailing off those rocks all the time. Nobody told us because we're kids and they're afraid it would put ideas into our heads."

Glen said, "Would you do it?"

"No, not us. I didn't mean that. It's not for us. It's for guys who got caught stealing money from the bank, or ladies whose babies died. That's the kind of people who need it." Tilden stood up and took a few steps toward the brink to illustrate. "You could spread your wings like one of those swifts. You could just lean over and swan dive in. It would be your greatest moment ever."

I recalled, "Some lady at our church killed herself because of cancer. Mom said she didn't blame her one bit."

"The Falls?"

"Shotgun."

"Ladies don't usually use shotguns."

"This one did."

Glen had been thinking hard about something. "You said there is a cave, a space."

"Has to be. Where else would all those swifts go?"

"Maybe they turn into fish."

"Maybe *you* turn into fish."

"We didn't see the bottom of the gorge," Glen went on.

"Not very well."

"Can't see it now anyhow."

"What if there's . . . I don't know what . . . what if there's a door there?"

"What do you mean a door?"

Glen arranged his face so it looked solemn in the birdy twilight. "What if it's the one place where there's a door out of the world, so you can go without having to die. So the people throwing themselves over don't die. They knock upon the water, and it opens, and they walk through the door and start again. Somewhere else."

We considered in silence.

Vince said, "Somebody would have to keep the big rocks out of the basin. They'd still kill you even if there was a magic door."

"Maybe somebody does."

A thought formed in my mind, a thought of such immensity I could barely get it out. "Maybe we will. We'll clear the rocks away. Maybe that's why we came here . . . why we were led here. Maybe we will be a secret society to keep the pool down there safe for all the sad divers."

I knew by their silence that they were, at least, considering it.

While we bent over stone cliffs watching the entrance of the swifts, the moon rose in his first quarter, blue-white, almost hurtful in the clear air, brilliant for all his slender newness. We stood. We worked the cricks out of our backs and necks. Vince put his arms around us from the back and lifted us, one at a time, the way he knew how to do, cracking our spines and making the blood flow again. It was so dark in the shadows cast by the moon that we wouldn't have known we were there, unless we knew. The bats probably could hear our thoughts with their sonar.

Tilden said, "The swifts leave too early in the morning for people to see. Usually it's still dark, so nobody bothers with that. But you can see it at the end, in the evening, like this. People come just for it, just to see the birds." He looked around to make sure. "I guess we're the only ones tonight. That's good. That's the best."

"How do you know all this?" Vince said.

Tilden answered, "Stands to reason."

Silence settled, except for the twittering of the swifts. Then, "Sons of bitches," said Tilden in a tone of awe.

Glen asked, "How many times you seen this?"

"Seven or eight," Vince replied. "It never gets old."

Glen said, "I want to live there."

"Where?" I said. "In the cave?"

"Yeah, in the cave under the falls. Where the birds go. I bet it's room after room. I bet it's a palace."

"You can't live there."

"Maybe you can't, but I can."

Tilden said, "It probably stinks of bird poop."

I don't think Glen heard him.

We decided we couldn't stay until the last birds came home. We couldn't see them anymore anyway, and the twittering we heard might be the settled-in birds singing in their sleep.

II

Wyona is a shy mountain boy, reluctant to leave home, rising from the smoky Carolina hills, flowing a little toward the Tennessee Valley, lingering with many a meander among the tulip poplars and sweet gums, looping back, delaying, uncertain, before squaring his shoulders and foaming bold toward the Gulf of Mexico. Once he makes up his mind he goes pretty fast, and our town, or rather the Falls below our town, is the place where he faces the inevitable and all his meandering turns to hurry, the Wyona to the Minangus, the Minangus to the Tennessee, and with all waters reaching the Great Water at last amid the herons and alligators of the Delta.

Sometimes the river is lazy. Mothers take their children to paddle in the shallows. Sometimes the river possesses terrible purpose, rooting under the mountains, swallowing barns, pushing towns on his back down toward the sea. The flood of 1916, when two hurricanes dumped their torrents at once, left its mark on walls and cliffs, so high that nobody believes there could be that much water on the dry land. Sometimes he plays like a big boy in the rocky shallows, and the gentlest thing can come to him and slake its thirst, the fledgling birds, and the blue-black butterflies that drink from a pool on a stone in a pool of the river bend.

It's possible to know a river longer than you've been alive, if your father knew it before you and his father knew it before him.

The river flows sad sometimes because everything changes and he alone remains the same. The river remembers when the industrial park over on 414 was a grove of trees. The river remembers boys shinnying up the waterside sycamores, who now sleep in the Baptist cemetery with the thrushes hymning them at evening. You could fall in love with the one at the barn dance you passed over your arm, and you would live with her until the day you died. In parlors, on dressing tables and dusty mantels, sit portraits of people whom nobody remembers but the river. They've sat there so long and people have dusted around them so long that they're part of the decor, and will not be moved until the last aunt dies and the house is sold to someone new moving uphill from the crowded cities. Everybody remembers something, and somebody remembers everything, and that's what knits the fibers of the world together.

Most of the stuff that happens when you're a kid doesn't bear mentioning because everyone has the same experiences. You hang out with your friends. You have teachers you hate and teachers you love. You long for a bike, and then for a car. You get into trouble. You discover interests. You flirt. You fumble with girls in the riverside parks after curfew. You see what lies ahead, and you either fight it or you relax into it. Growing up how we did, it was easy to relax into it. It's what our dads had done. The ways were wide and paved. The War had been fought and old boring Europe lay in ruins. Now there was only us. Given all that, it's easy to forgive us for thinking it had all been planned out pretty well. Honey poured upon your fingers, and all you had to do was bend your neck and lick.

My big brother Andy had seen the last months of the European war, driving up into Italy behind General Clark, learning a little Italian which he used when he was with girls. He didn't need it: handsome dog, my brother was. Before he went away, Andy hung out with us sometimes, occasions which we cherished and tried not to anticipate, like some extra gift under the tree Christmas morning. They let him come home a little while. Leave couldn't have been much fun if you had to think about going back to the war, but Andy made the best of it. He removed the uniform the minute he walked through the door, and wore the white T-shirt and tan pants he'd worn before, except that the pants were too big and the T-shirt a little small now in the chest, he had become such a man.

One day he said, "Come on." I didn't need a second invitation. Wherever he led I was going to follow. He said, "Bring the other two Stooges as well," and I spent about ten minutes rounding up the gang while Andy had a little breakfast. This was before Glen came.

Mom told Andy, "You be careful now."

Andy smiled at her. They'd just bombed Monte Cassino right over his head, for God's sake. I guess, though, there's things in the woods that there's not even in the war, and Mom knew about them. Andy would be careful.

Ended up we were going up Godwallow Creek to where it spreads out under the sourwood trees. Andy went slow, looking at everything like he might never see it again. We went slow behind him. That we might not see anything again never crossed our minds, so we were a little impatient. Tilden began naming the trees and flowers, like he did sometimes. He was good at that. It made a nice contrast to his cussing.

We'd been there before, but I guess we didn't know what we should have been looking for, because when Andy began to flip over rocks at creek side, salamanders slid out of them, in a dozen different colors—the regular ones like you'd expect, brown and black, but also orange and spotted orange and olive and almost blue. Andy knew the names of some of them. When a kind of salamander appeared and he didn't call out the name, you knew he didn't know the name, and he was amazed as us at the bounty the waters and the mountain could keep exuding. As we moved up Godwallow, other little creeks poured into it. Clearly the salamanders changed as the creeks did, since every ravine and hollow had its own kind. We were splashing around in a kind of salamander town square where they all met for a little while and sampled the local bug supplies, and maybe courted like the high school kids, if that's what salamanders do. Tilden actually knew a little about salamanders—as he knew a little about every creepy crawler you could think of—and, slowly and very politely, began to fill in the blanks where Andy's knowledge flagged. Whenever it seemed like Andy was going to say something, you could hear our flytraps slamming shut. We wanted to hear everything. We wanted him to tell us about the war and bazookas and what the Germans were like, but he never satisfied us on those points. He'd talk about the mountain and the salamanders, though, and we caught on that he was filling his mind with them so the war and the Germans could be washed out the other side.

I tried to be just a stupid kid. That's how Andy remembered me. That's what he needed from me right then.

Andy was bigger than us, but a small kid for his age. Mom called him "compact." I loved being with him, but had learned it was more profitable to wait for him to make the offer than to try to tag along when he was with his friends. The army changed him. He'd always been serious, the sober one of his gang. Now he was downright solemn some of the time. You'd hear him say something like it was church, and turn around to see a kid in a T-shirt with a solemn look on his face. It was a disconnect. He'd have long talks with Dad, and once I could hear one of them crying. His buddies all went to the war somewhere, so he had to hang out with us by default, I guess.

Only part of the war was over at the time. He had to go back. Still, that day was one of the golden ones. Curiously incurious as a boy, I thought those matters worth investigation were all in books. As often as I'd been to Godwallow Creek, it had never occurred to me to ask how it got its name, or where it came from, or where it went. Where it came from was the easiest told, for it descended like a narrow carpet down hard stairs made of the stones of the mountain, from nearly the very top, Andy said, getting quite agitated in places, pooling out into nice calm ponds good for fishing in others. "A big old hemlock got blown over and lies on its side," Andy said, "way up there, way higher than you'd think a hemlock would ever grow. The tree got blown over, and out of the hole its roots left bubbled Godwallow. The tree is still alive, too, its branches twisting around like little trees to get back to the vertical. The creek keeps it alive."

"There was no creek before the tree fell?" Vince asked.

"Must have been. I never saw it, is all."

"You saw this tree?"

"Yep."

"How far?"

"Farther than I want to go today."

We all pictured a creek liberated from some subterranean world by the fall of a tree, like champagne popping from a bottle. Andy led us to one of the wide pools, the biggest we'd found yet, with a black oozy bottom from generations of fallen sourwood leaves. Sassafras leaned over in spots where more light struck, dipping close to the water with its three leaves like three different hands. The pool was not often—perhaps never—fished, and rippled with fins and the loud smack of fish taking bugs on the surface. Andy said, "Here," and hove his backpack onto a rock at the side of the pool.

"So where does it go?" Vince asked.

"What?"

"Godwallow Creek."

I knew this one. I said, "We're on the western side of the Continental Divide. It all goes to the Gulf of Mexico."

Andy said, "But first it goes to the Wyona. Right under the Picnic Bridge. Then over the—"

"Over the what?"

"Nothing." We didn't know about the Falls then, and he wasn't going to tell us. Instead, he said, "Start lifting up anything flat, that something big could live under."

Vinny wasn't all that interested in wildlife, though he was interested abstractly in the hunt and in lifting heavy objects, so he became the official rock-turner. He'd wait for us to situate ourselves in a place where our bodies would shade the water from the glare of the sun, then he'd hoist the rock and let us see what dwelt under it. Crawdads, predominately, but leeches and bugs and stuff, the occasional snake, which would scare me witless and make me scream like a girl. Vince liked lifting the heavy ones, and though Andy explained the big ones were not necessarily the likeliest choices, he went to the rocks that Vince was set to lift, it was clearly making him so happy. We were standing against the light and ready, when Vince began to tug on a flat white stone that proved considerably weightier than it appeared. It went down deep, half in the mud and half in the water, and while he was lifting, Vince breathed out, "This is the one! This is the one!"

I don't know how he knew, but it was, in fact, the one. Vince got the rock vertical before we saw squirming movement in the water. My first impulse was to scream the snake scream, but the motion wasn't serpentine. Not a snake. What we thought at first was something really big was actually two black bodies, writhing around in the black water. Had they stayed still we would never have seen them at all. The first one darted between my legs and out into the pool. It was lizard-shaped, but blunter, fetus-like. It moved like nothing I was familiar with. It scared me and I was afraid to pick it up. The other body made for the same gap, but Tilden stepped into the pool and headed it off, grabbing past me and bringing the creature out of the water. It was as long as his forearm, struggling and whacking his chest wet with its flat tail. It was a hellbender. We would have called it by that name even if we had never heard it before. It regarded us with tiny, primeval, expressionless eyes. It was magnificent.

Tilden held the giant salamander so it couldn't bite him. It didn't look like it was inclined to bite, but you never knew. It looked like the warmth of Tilden's body was something of a comfort. A ripple went through its long body, a cold, muscular contraction that made Tilden make a face and say,

"Eww." Vince stood right up to it, eye to eye. I looked on from a safe, though scientifically engaged, distance. Andy looked less at the hellbender than at us, pretty well satisfied. The creature itself looked at the blue dome of sky, which it probably didn't see that much.

Tilden ventured, "Maybe it's a salamander scientist, and lured us up here just so he could get a good look at us." It was, in fact, scrutinizing us with disturbing concentration.

Vince said, "We ain't keeping it."

"Naw," Tilden answered. He lowered the creature back toward the water. It moved nothing but its head, which it raised to keep the same angle of perspective it had on us before.

Vince got out of the water and lowered the rock back down, so the hellbenders would have their shelter to return to. When the rock settled back down, Tilden released the animal. He didn't surge away the way you'd expect, but balanced himself for a moment on Tilden's boot. Then he blended his body with the water, and was instantly invisible.

Tilden said, "I felt him. I felt him push off my boot into the pool!"

We stared at the motionless water. Except for the spinning water bugs, there was no sign that anything dwelt there at all.

Andy said, "We'd never have seen them unless they wanted us to."

Our four shadows went still over the stillest water in the world. Then Andy added, "That goes for damn near everything."

Going home I realized what all that had been about, why Andy wanted to take us to Godwallow Creek. Whatever was happening in the world, on the day of the hellbenders there was perfect peace.

Glen came that fall. Whenever I mentioned Andy, Glen said, "Who?" This irritated me no end. Then I remembered he hadn't been there. He hadn't seen the hellbenders. I gave a lot of thought to why we should have seen the hellbenders and Glen not. The mind of a child is symbolic and speculative and "because he didn't live here then" did not suffice. I took him out there once, to Godwallow Creek, to the same pool Andy had shown us. We grunted big slabs of wet rock high into the air, but there were no hellbenders. This disturbed me. I remarked on it and Glen said the right thing. He said, "Probably Andy is a little magic and that's why you saw them then."

"Yes," I thought, "exactly."

For a while we were almost indistinguishable, Tilden and Glen and Vince and I, until freshman year and football entered our lives for real. Vince separated out pretty quickly. He played every minute of the JV games. We thought it was because his dad was Coach Silvano, "Big Vince," but after a while we had grudgingly to admit he was pretty good. No, Tilden and I were pretty good; Vince was a phenomenon. Coach Silvano seemed hard and cruel to us, and not much interested in his only son, so when Vince began to put us in second position behind the one thing that should have made his papa proud, we understood. Football came first from then on.

We played at my house—Vince's mom had "headaches"—so I didn't know Coach that well until we began to learn football from him. He was skillful and mean and unfair and often cruel, but I was in love with him for a while.

All the boys were. Many of us went through a hard-ass stage in his honor, only to have it beaten out of us by someone we admired even more later on, a mother or a girlfriend or a best buddy who had seen enough. We wanted to be praised by Coach. We wanted to be Coach. His son had to want the same things, with fiercer desire even than the rest of us. Coach was good at what he did. He won over schools a lot bigger than ours. People took lot of shit from him without ever calling it "shit." Coach Silvano was the one thing our town had that resembled a permanent celebrity.

Glen came at almost the same moment football did. Glen was like a stone dropped in a pond—a thing that makes a disturbance for a while, then blends in to the quiet scene as though nothing had happened. Vince had always been my best friend, and we never varied in that. But I recognized Glen and Vince had a connection I didn't quite understand. I thought it was that Glen was a bit of a spaz, and Vince felt protective. I hoped it was that. Tilden was the lowest maintenance person anybody ever met, and whether he was ever jealous or uncomfortable it was impossible to tell. Even his cussing was gentle, a kind of benediction particular to him.

Coach was very big on not being a homo. I had, at first, no idea what he was talking about when he talked about that. We did not associate "homo" with human affection of any kind. A homo was someone who was not on the football squad, someone in the marching band or the choir or a reader of unassigned material or one who took art class beyond the requirement. Glen fit into a number of these categories. That something more loomed behind "homo" was a gradual discovery. I credit full exploration of the term with releasing me from Big Vince's spell a little quicker than most.

Andy was back at the front for, like, two days when he got shot and had to convalesce in a hospital in Pisa. He sent me a photo of a big red hole in his left side, him turning his head and grinning at the camera like he'd just won a prize at the fair. I was a hero at school for his sake for a couple of days. The assistant principal, Mr. Jay (a homo, according to Coach), appeared at practice and told Coach that the halftime festivities would be extended a little on Friday to recognize my brother for receiving the Purple Heart. We all cheered, but Coach narrowed his eyes. He always narrowed his eyes when he thought the spotlight was going to shift, however briefly, from himself and his squad. He said, "Jesus God, are we going to have to line up and salute every time some homo gets himself in the line of fire?" He looked around to make sure the boys were laughing at his witticism, and some of them did. I didn't. That broke the Coach spell for me.

For a couple of years we tested one another's mettle by doing a polar bear camp along the Wyona just above the Falls, where the slopes faced north and we imagined it would be colder and rougher. We slept all jumbled in a heap, like puppies in a box. We prided ourselves on traveling light, but Glen had a Boy Scout pack that his mother had sewn patches on, and he would not hike without it, being that a Boy Scout needs to "Be Prepared" and all that. There was no Scout troop within thirty miles, so Glen had to carry on the tradition all by his lonesome, a "Lone Wolf," a pursuit which made him even more conspicuous than usual. He'd have to wear his uniform when he was doing Scout stuff, and if that didn't make him a target, nothing would. But in that pack he managed to carry the things we found ourselves in need of but were too proud to bear, matches or extra socks or a Three Musketeers bar or what have you. We rolled our eyes when we saw it on him, but praised him silently when it saved our butts.

On one of those nights—an unusually bitter Thanksgiving weekend—I saw something I had no experience, then, to understand. I was spooning Tilden, his tough little body curled against mine facing the dim, red, still flickering campfire. I hoped I'd wake him so we could trade places—my back was freezing against the river with its winds and sprays—but when I sat up, not all the way, just a little, I saw that Vince and Glen were not spooning. They lay face to face. They were kissing like people in the movies, gentle and hungry at once, passionate, transfigured, no longer boys. Vince moaned a little, like Glen was hurting him, but I knew he wasn't. I felt . . . I didn't know what I felt right then, but when I analyzed later, I knew I felt left out. Vince and Glen had forged ahead where I was not ready to go. With me it would be a girl, but I didn't suppose the basics were that much different. I wondered when I would want somebody so much I'd groan on a frozen hillside.

I could tell by the movement he made that Tilden was awake, too, watching.

I heard Tilden whisper, "Are we supposed to do that?"

I waited before I answered. I really didn't know, so I said, "I don't know. You want to?"

Tilden waited a very long time. Finally he said, "Naw." He snuggled back against me where it was all warm and comfy—for him. Changing places would cause too much upheaval now, so I just settled into it and tried to get back to sleep.

III

One time Glen came to my house with a long roll of paper. He wouldn't say what it was; he would only show me, so we tramped down into the basement, and when he unrolled the paper on the ping-pong table, it turned out to be a map of the world. On the Europe part, he had traced in colored pens the engagements of Andy's company up from Sicily into Italy, with places Andy had mentioned in his letters marked by blue stars. He painted a big star over Pisa (I'd never bothered to find out where Pisa was) where Andy was at that point healing up from being shot by the Jerries. I called Mom and Dad down. Dad picked the map up—the spread of his arms was not quite enough to straighten it out flat in the air—and stared at it for a long time, his nose a mere inch from the blue Mediterranean. After he put it back on the ping-pong table, Mom smoothed it out and traced with her fingers the travels of her firstborn. They said nothing. They didn't have to. But before Glen left, Dad poked his head back down the stairs and said, "Thank you," in a tone you didn't hear that often.

So it was the night Glen informed us of a fire in the sky. It was a Glen thing, and therefore suspect, but how cool if true! For a few delicious moments we assumed that was what he really meant, that a great blaze from above was going to end the world, until he went into his lecture on space debris and the coming to earth of some in a shower called the Leonids. Meteors is what he meant, after all. Not the Apocalypse, but good enough. Mom drove us out to the Knoxville Highway to find us a place to watch the meteors. At some later time she would honk three times to tell us she was there with the car to take us home.

Glen settled down in the night grass, lying on his back, looking up into the billion billion stars. The trees on three sides of the highway pull-over stood still and gray in the darkness, but now that I've said "gray" I have to add that they were also stone black below and luminous coppery silver above, where they fronted the sky. The fourth side was a wall of stars. Glen's head rested on the palms of his hands, the long gray stalks of the mountain grass poking up beside his elbows and knees. He was silent. He was happy. I could tell though it was too dark to see his face very well. I wasn't sure he was looking at the sky, or at me, or at Vince—who was teetering along the curb like an Olympic balance beam contestant—or if he was looking at anything at all. Enough light issued from the stars that I could see his smile and the outline of his body. It seemed strange to me that a kid who wanted to see the stars so much, who'd made such a point of being there in time for the show, would be lying down on the grass, rather than standing up with me, closer to the sky, on the slope of the mountain, as near heaven as you can get around here. The minute I thought that, though, I realized how silly it was, to count a few inches in the face of the immensities between us and those points of light.

If one actually fell, if a meteor fell out of the sky, it would annihilate us all in the same second.

A little breeze came, and the dark and light and the leaves and the grass stirred around us like millions of decks of cards shuffled by invisible dealers. When the breeze was right you could hear sounds, sometimes human voices, sometimes the stirring of animals, from the purple-blackness below the hill, where there were a few farms and long stretches of forest. The lights of the farms made the surrounding emptiness that much darker.

Tilden was singing in the blue darkness. Tilden had a nice voice, but it was the sort of thing you'd never say to him. If you mentioned he had a nice voice he'd know you had heard him, and the fiction, shared wordlessly, tacitly among us, was that Tilden's singing was private and inaudible, heard only by himself. He made up the tunes, I think, or if he didn't, he was listening to a different radio station than the rest of us. It was a shame. He sounded good, but we already anticipated running with a crowd in the midst of which one never sang to oneself.

The point of honor that night was to be the first to see a shooting star. "November, the Leonids," Glen said, a night when the sky would fill with shooting stars like a battle scene in a space movie. I saw one as soon as we parked, but Glen said it didn't count because it was too early and it wasn't a Leonid but a plain old meteor. There was no use arguing with Glen when he'd made up his mind about something like that.

I looked at him lying belly up in the grass.

"You happy?"

"What?"

"Are you happy, Glen?"

"I guess so. You?"

"I'd be happier if you counted my meteor."

"It counts as a meteor but not as a Leonid. I thought I explained that."

"Why do you get to decide?"

Glen shrugged. That's just the way it was.

Vince said, "What are you girls talking about?" and squeezed in between us, so our skinny boy bodies were wedged together like sardines in a can.

"I was just asking why Glen gets to decide everything."

Vince thought a minute and said, "Because he's smarter than me and Tilden doesn't really care. That just leaves you bitchin' and moanin' like an old woman."

I took his point and turned my attention to the stars. Restless Tilden started chasing lightning bugs. I could feel the sudden cold where his body left the proximity of mine. The three of us were lying on our backs with heads resting on our hands. We weren't the only people to know about the meteorites, so every now and then a car ground into the pull-over, sweeping the stars away with its headlights. As our eyes readjusted, we listened to the conversations of the newcomers, couples, mostly, taking the excuse of scientific observation for a night together in the woods. The boy-girl couple just up the hill from us had gotten there before we did, and were a little bored, and were beginning to play with each other, and giggle, and admonish each other, "Watch the sky, now." A white van pulled up below with a bunch of kids in it, older kids, maybe college kids. They were drunk, but sweet and happy. One big kid flopped down into the grass beside Glen. I don't think he knew he was there; I think he thought Glen was a natural feature, a gray swelling out of the gray rock of the mountain. He liked it that way.

We hoped that when people died they became part of the mountain, and never quite left the scenes of their lives. That's why the mountains were so big. They keep growing and what they grow with is us. We liked that.

I looked up again at the twinkling dome. Mom taught me to wish on a star once, but I forgot the exact procedure. Glen would know. I figured he was wishing a lot harder and a lot more than me anyway. He was one of those people who had an emptiness in him that wasn't meanness or sin or anything like that, but just strangeness, as if he hadn't figured himself out yet. Of course he would be wishing for something I couldn't comprehend. Maybe he was wishing to be a girl so he could have Vince the way he had him that night at the camp-out. I was still trying to figure out how all that might work in the life before us. Me, I was actually pretty content as I understood things. Vince claimed victory on every field and Tilden lived in a world of his own making. None of us would answer questions like, "Are you happy?" when we thought they were serious, so there was no use asking. We were all right.

A car approached, hesitated, went on higher up the mountain. A big hoot-owl went at it down in the darkness, *who-who*-ing in a way which would have been scary if my pals hadn't been with me.

Some of the voices coming out of the night were more familiar than others. We heard a couple of Coach's boys, a couple of the younger footballers. We would have joined them, maybe, had Glen not sunk down in the grass like he was a tortoise trying to find a shell to hide in. They were just JV's from the middle school, but Coach's influence had reached down to them, and they would be particular about whom they ran with, and cruel to those they didn't.

I was about to say, "I'm getting bored," when, almost at the limits of visibility, Tilden's arm shot out straight, pointing at the sky. I looked up at the glimmering remnant of a meteor's trail. I was about to remark on how interesting that was when another came, and another. I admit I thought we weren't going to see anything. It wasn't until other people gathered in the darkness, looking up expectantly into the star-bowl, that I realized the Leonids were not a Glen Copland invention.

People around us were saying "Ah!" I looked up again at the dark sky slashed with white trails of flame. Ten, twenty, forty, a storm of falling rock transformed into a lace of pale fire. Glen lay on the ground with his arms open, welcoming the shooting stars. Without moving my head, I could see the fire trails appearing low in the east, but mostly I was looking at Glen, his arms held up like that. I'd seen that gesture before, in a book or a slide show, or maybe a sleeping bag on the side of a mountain. Glen had taken the sky as his lover. The gesture was too knowing: I didn't think the sky was his first.

"Glen?" Vince said.

"Yeah?"

"Doesn't this just make you come in your pants?"

Glen's arms collapsed onto his chest, his hands contracted into fists. He bent in the middle a little, lifting his back off the turf. He let out this spluttering wheeze which is what happens when a good one catches you off guard. He seized a deep breath, and then his belly-laugh belled out over the mountain silence—strange how silent it was, when the meteors were so like fireworks you expected explosions midair—and you could see the shadows of people turning to look at him, but you knew it was all good, that the sound was somehow exactly right, Copland holding his belly, his eyes mere slits now, tears streaming from the corners, as the shooting stars blazed and went out, blazed and went out.

"I swear to God, Silvano," he said when he could catch his breath.

The couple just above us might have come to see the shooting stars, but they were doing something else now. The little flashlight they brought to look at the star map had gone out. One could hear her low moans as he fumbled about in her shirt, under the loosened top of her jeans. That was the last November when sex was still funny to me.

The meteor flashes slowed a little over the ridge, but if you looked east they were still coming like a fake-out bomb attack, all fizzle and no bang, beautiful, the way artillery must be if you know it will never hit its mark. I didn't know if you were supposed to be afraid or not, but the comparisons I made in my imagination to cannon and artillery made me apprehensive.

"What if it did?" I said out loud. "What if one of those things actually made it to the ground? Glen? What if it did?"

Glen took a minute to consider this. He sat up. I could see the sticks and leaves clinging to the back of his gray sweatshirt. Finally he said, "That would be so goddamn beautiful."

IV

I was already in the water, already up to my neck in Green's Pond when Vinny comes striding out of the woods buck naked, his shorts and T-shirt wadded in his hand. Vince was growing blond hair under his arms and in a line up from his dick toward his belly button. You could see the down fluttering a little in the wind, almost invisible, but not quite, for a person who was really looking.

"Hey, Arden?"

"What?"

"You playing with yourself down there under the water?"

"No."

"Let me see your hands."

I raised my hands to show I was not playing with myself, or had at least left off doing so. Vince nodded, acknowledging it was, therefore, safe to come in.

"I know something cool," he said. He shuddered a little as the first frigid water hit his balls. He'd forgotten the clothes in his hand, and tossed them backward toward the shore without even looking where they might have landed. They hit a dry stone a few inches off shore. He was miraculous that way.

"What?" I said.

"We're going to have a new teacher. First thing in the fall."

Fresh hires were rare in our district. They had to be Christians, but not too vocal about it. They should go to covered-dish suppers but not make altar call more than once a year. It would help if they were local, though over the years "local" had expanded to include most of western Carolina and eastern Tennessee. They should be female, unless they were a coach. Married men were sometimes considered, but it struck the citizens as peculiar when a grown man would settle for what the district had to pay. This time all the signifiers were aligned. We were among the first in the know because adults were always talking in front of Coach's kid like he was one of them.

It gave us a thrill to sneak into the school office, sashay casually past the Teachers' Assignment Board, and discover that our new teacher's given name was Nancy. Teachers' first names were as taboo at that point as names of sexual organs. We whispered them one to another like guilty secrets. The name "Nancy" seemed wonderfully old-fashioned; amid the throng of Dianes and Karens and Susans in our class, there had never once, from kindergarten on, been a Nancy. It was an old lady's name, an Edwardian girls' adventure novel name, and that's what we expected that hot and crabby day after Labor Day when we began our sixth year of elementary school. "Old Lady McWhirter" already nestled comfortably on our tongues.

It was a waste of malice, for Nancy McWhirter was younger than any of our parents, younger than some of our older sisters. Her car still bore an Appalachian State University student parking sticker. She cut her brown haircut at a severe angle across her forehead, maybe a little over-styled, but very adult, and with a sophistication meant to belie her youth. Those in the know recognized the cut as one girls got when they meant to be taken for professionals.

Sixth grade is not as hard on teachers as some. But Nancy was new, and different from us in ways that opened her up to opposition that a local could have avoided. She did better than anybody could expect. Some of the girls hated her instantly; many took her on as model and confidante. Most of the boys were gaga. I was, I know, in my way. Our boy Tilden, however, was miles beyond the rest of us in being smitten with Nancy McWhirter.

A crush made me elaborately polite, over-enunciating my words as though courtesy and clarity were the way to a person's heart. Tilden was more old-school. He blathered and drooled and tripped over his own feet. Tilden was annihilated. Tilden was in real love, a different love from mine—which was, now that I think of it, really an advanced form of ass-kissing. He took love the way a boxer takes a blow to the gut, with a single *oof*, and then the kind of silence only produced by a man who thinks the next sound must be singing. Vince and I were the only ones who knew how bad it was for him. As we became adolescents, our ability to smooth the real emotions from our face had become almost eerie. Tilden moaned when he thought no one was listening. He purred like a sleeping cat. He sang songs from the radio deep under his breath, and when we asked him what he was doing he inevitably answered, "Nothing." Tilden in love was odder than ordinary Tilden, which was odd enough, and even his best friends didn't know what to do for him.

Mom made me swear a solemn vow not to make fun of Tilden over his affections, and after initial disappointment, I saw her point. We were reticent about Nancy McWhirter around Tilden. This allowed him to think nobody knew how his heart was cloven in twain. This allowed him to act out his drama in a state that he, endearingly, assumed was totally invisible.

For a month or so, Tilden walked forth in a cloud of cologne, with his hair combed, with all the buttons of his shirt inserted in their proper buttonhole. I don't know who was giving him advice on matters of fashion. One of those old Arrow shirt ads, maybe. His dad was a sharp-dressed man, but Tilden's style turned out to be his own, a little more casual than his dad's subtle, autodidact preppie. Eventually the waves of cologne went away, and Tilden became merely well-bathed, an example to us all.

I don't know how Tilden got over Nancy McWhirter. Maybe he never did.

One of Miss McWhirter's first innovations was to replace *Anne of Green Gables* in the syllabus with a "classic." Sixth graders had been subjected to *Anne of Green Gables* time out of mind. Parents were used to it. Administrators felt safe with it. Students sighed and accepted it as an inevitability. Store rooms were stacked with well-thumbed copies poised to be used again. The way was paved, the gates wide open for *Anne of Green Gables*. Why, everyone wondered when the change was announced, couldn't people just go along with the plan? But Miss McWhirter was new and smarter than everybody, as the new usually are, and she was having none of it.

I didn't know what a classic was, but I knew my mom was bent out of shape by it. Somebody organized a big meeting at school one night, and Mom and Dad went and had their say. Rickenbacker Elementary had not stood one block from the town square for sixty years to have a brand new teacher from out of town change the syllabus just because she thought kids should have exposure to the greatest literature in the world. Wiser heads than hers had steered a course between violence and suggestibility and arrived at the perfect scholarly menu: bland, but, in some demonstrable way, nourishing. The parents of the girls were especially upset about losing *Anne of Green Gables*. I haven't read it to this day, but I gathered the hero was a girl, or that some heroic part was played by a girl, or a girl dies or something, and it was real important for girls to have suchlike role-modeling at that time in their lives. This alone was enough to throw me into the classic camp. Miss McWhirter was persuasive, and just as the leaves were turning yellow and red, we found on our desks bright blue copies of the *Iliad* of Homer. In the center of the bright blue was the black silhouette of a studly warrior in a plumed helmet, about to hurl a javelin. We had to file up to the front of the room to get our copies. As he did, every single boy examined the cover, stopped, and briefly assumed the position of the midnight warrior, invisible javelins aimed at the playing field outside the windows. The girls might have looked glancingly at the cover, but they did not, not even one of them, Amazon themselves in a like manner. This gained a place among the puzzlements of my youth. Did girls get together and vow not to react to the warrior if the boys did? Did they all pick their books up upside down and fail to notice the warrior was there? I posed the problem to my mom, and she said, "Boys and girls are different," as if that weren't the one fragment of information I had already.

Had I known what the *Iliad* was about, I'd not have been so neutral an observer; I'd have been at school shouting down my own parents. The book was great. Even if it was a poem, it was amazing, the best movie ever, except you could go back to your favorite parts again and again. The men were all strapping adults, but with an exposed edge to their passions, a petty persistence to their grievances that any eleven year old could recognize and admire. It's practically a manual on how a middle school boy should conduct himself.

The price Miss McWhirter paid for victory was that she agreed to use a kids' version of the poem, one with a lot of the gore left out. This ended up having an effect opposite to the one intended, for as soon as we discovered there was a more brutal version, we launched ourselves down to the library to find it, or scoured the shelves for our parents' old college texts, to read the original, guiltily hidden under blankets in the watches of the night, in tree houses, garages, all such places of seclusion that sixth graders have access to. Consider for a moment the phenomenon of American schoolchildren sneaking around trying to get surreptitious glimpses of Homer. I think Miss McWhirter had it planned from the first. She had that look on her face of one who was inviting you to a violin recital, and we all made the faces, but she alone knew it was actually a demolition derby, and we'd have our coats off shouting in five minutes. These Greek guys were all the time getting spears through their viscera and falling down into the dust, lamenting their lost youth. It was, as I said, amazing.

I don't know that discussions of the *Iliad* of Homer marked the first time Vince raised his hand and offered an observation in English class, but it certainly hadn't been a daily occurrence. He hit the mark, too, in what he said, and kids in the room turned to look at him, to make sure they'd recognized the voice correctly. The general level of enthusiasm in class was, for a while, so high that anyone with a working familiarity with the local school system could have guessed that Miss McWhirter's chances of being retained were slim. Any pedagogy that loudly successful was bound to be a threat to the tenured "experts," every minute of whose classes were a lead weight around the necks of their students. At one point when we were hanging out at Tilden's, his mom suggested that we put down our homework and go outdoors and play. The three of us stared at one another for a moment after the utterance, realizing that something had been said which had never been said before, and which was very unlikely ever to be said again.

Long experience as the Coach's son had taught Vince to keep his uncertain enthusiasms cloaked, not to call attention to himself off the field when it could be avoided. What if he liked something creepy or girly? He could not afford to be caught unawares in matters like that. But the *Iliad* set him off in ways not to be controlled. Miss McWhirter refused to pronounce any of the jaw-cracking names until we'd at least given it a try, and Vince saved us hours of embarrassed silence by blazing out with "Agamemnon" and "Philoctetes" like they were his next door neighbors. I could see his body shift and change as he read, taking on the posture of the heroes, the aggressive forward lunge of Hector with his outstretched sword, the hesitating glamour of Helen on the ramparts, the upright, massy weightlessness of the gods on Olympus. It was a gigantic adventure movie and he got to play all the parts.

Tilden was in love with the teacher and Vince with the text. It was a home run for elementary education.

The boys came over to my house in the evening so we could read the story together. Vince had to arrange the light in the room just so, the sun sinking on the wine-dark sea, or some such. Tilden made fun of his high seriousness, but never refused any of the stage directions Vince constantly supplied. Sometimes Vince would be blind Homer, intoning in a voice he pitched as low as he could, which was considerable, as his voice had always been amazingly, not to say freakishly, low. Mom came upstairs just to check who all crowded in my bedroom, with the bardic voice booming and rustling. Tilden took his turn reading, but he was a little halting, and you could tell Vince was squirming with impatience the whole time, so Tilden's passages got progressively shorter and Vince's longer, as if anybody cared. Tilden was great at sound effects, the whistle of arrows through the shining air, the thud of spear heads against bone.

Vince's transformation was the most remarkable when he got to the parts about the gods. I went to Sunday school, and had a little trouble with the concept of gods who were not Jesus, but Vince took to them like a pagan born. When Zeus the Thunderer had his entrance, Vince marched around making thunder noises and lightning noises, a tempest there in my room. When it was Athena, he made himself straight and bright-eyed, his arm bent in front of him in a way I eventually recognized as her holding a giant shield. It was Apollo, though, who really got to him. It was funny to see Vince become Apollo, with his little belly sticking out and his skinny arms held out like rays of light were dripping from them. Vince let us laugh, but I don't think it was all that funny to him. He had found a role model. It would be difficult to imagine a tougher one than the god of light. General Patton or Captain America were well within reach by comparison.

Winter came, and the snow forts with it—on those rare occasions when the snow was sufficient for them at all—were no longer Alamos or Fort Apaches, but the walls of Troy. The branches of the playground trees became the watchtowers of Ilium, from which could be descried the hosts of the Achaeans arising from the sea. Vince would have to remind us that we were no longer shooting the long rifles of the pioneers or launching the grenades of Audie Murphy, but hurling javelins and shooting arrows. This change of image improved our aim and accuracy considerably. I thought of this in later years when my passing arm whipped out like a pistol shot. When the reporters asked me "What's your secret, Summers?" I planned to say, "Throwing spears from the walls of Troy." It would be worth going pro just to have that opportunity.

Not only was I actually into a Greek poem from three thousand years ago, but that Christmas, instead of toys, I received things a young man not too far from middle school could use: a matched brush and comb set, an expensive chess set which was not red and black plastic like the one Vince and I took up into the tree house, but onyx and ivory, so weighty and substantial I thought it might really be onyx and ivory, and the bottoms of the pieces were covered in green felt to keep them from scratching the board.

Something clearly was in the water, a Homeric strain which turned boys into demigods. Maybe it was just puberty's first shots across our bows, but whatever it was inspired us to actions which astonished even ourselves. I fought Chuck Leggett in the locker room—Chuck who had been tormenting me since we were in kindergarten—and chipped two of his front teeth. Vince beat all the middle school boys at the high hurdles, and because nobody believed it, beat them again half an hour later with everybody from two schools watching. Tilden did three hundred sit-ups without stopping and got his name affixed in bronze to the gymnasium wall.

But beyond any of this ranked Vince's second deed of daring. Given a hundred tries we wouldn't have guessed what was coming.

He decided to try out for the school talent show.

Glen bears responsibility for this. Glen was in a different English class ("Advanced") and didn't have McWhirter and they read *The Scarlet Letter*. You could see Glen pulling Hawthorne out of his Boy Scout knapsack and reading at the lunch table, which was not done by anybody else, ever. You could throw a potato at him and he would not put down that book. Tilden and I didn't always know what went on between Glen and Vince—they took time to themselves in a way no other combination of us did—so whatever conversation or double-dare led to Vince's decision to veer toward the arts we never knew.

We were able to counsel him against choir or pep band. It's not that anyone would think that Coach's son was a homo if he joined the pep band, but it would have just been too baffling for the masses. People like Vince Silvano simply were not in bands or glee clubs, and when they were, it would be the time to rethink too much too fast. Tilden and I were still working on the problem when announcements were made for the annual talent show. Vince tried out—I didn't know then with what: free throws? weightlifting?—and made it.

News of Silvano in the talent show encouraged everyone to assume a goof. Surely he was having one over on the school. He had to be. Everyone with an older brother or sister remembered the year they elected horrific Jane Osterman as freshman attendant to the homecoming court. She was not just the ugliest girl in that class, but maybe the ugliest girl anyone had ever heard of. She was sweet, though, and chosen by the gods to possess a sense of humor strong enough to survive her appearance. The thing was that Jane wanted it. She wanted to be on the homecoming court. What girl didn't? The teachers got together and explained to her, as gently as they could, that it was meant as a joke. Jane already knew that—she had a mirror, for godssake—but she wanted it anyhow. She wanted to stand up there with Mark Crimaldi, the one-freshman-on-varsity stud, with her bouquet and little coronet, beaming into the cameras. Eventually the teachers nixed it, and let I-forget-who—some pretty girl who had come in, in fact, third—stand on the podium with Mark. That was a shame in so many ways. Like I just said, I forget who the substitute beauty was; nobody would have forgotten that year or that dance if Jane Osterman had been the freshman attendant.

Anyway, I was not immune to the camp buzz, and on the night of the talent show Tilden and I went to see our buddy perform, and we went prepared to laugh. I sat with the JV team in our white sweaters with sky blue letters—most of whom were present in support of their interpretive-dancing or guitar-strumming girlfriends—and waited for Vince to cause a stir. An odd thing about Vince was that everyone expected him to be the class clown; everyone expected him to goof on the serious matters the teachers laid before us, but he wasn't and he almost never did. It must have been that look on his face, that archaic smile which looked insolent to people looking for insolence. His beauty was so great that people assumed he was as involved in thoughts of himself as they were. He was good-humored, but I don't think you'd call him humorous. Vince could mouth off but he couldn't tell a decent joke. His deadpan was lethal, but not always intentional.

The theme of the talent show was "Around the World in Eighty Days," and the opening extravaganza involved the whole cast sashaying on stage singing that song, from an old movie or something, and there Vince was, not at the front, but not at the back either, warbling his heart out. You'd be disappointed trying to catch him in a smile of collusion. He was serious as cancer. And, God, he was handsome. Maybe his talent would be just standing there.

I figured the teachers had final pick of the numbers, as most of them were old. The Dawes sisters sang "Volare," which was supposed to be Italy, and this big girl from ninth grade sang "A Nightingale Sang in Berkeley Square," which was pretty good, and meant to invoke London, where Berkeley Square is. You saw her in the hall but you never knew she could sing. Ann Dadlez, the police chief's granddaughter, had been a Junior Miss runner-up, and she was supposed to sing "Spanish Eyes," the song that had wowed the Junior Miss judges, but Mrs. Hunt stood up from the piano bench and announced that Ann had the flu and could not appear tonight. A bunch of hoods did an Apache dance to "The Hawaiian War Chant," and it was actually amazing, those dark souls dancing like that. Their brothers and sisters had been to the gay clubs in Knoxville and taught them some snaky moves. They left everybody way behind, in terms of cool.

Vince came on first after intermission. We scurried back from the bathrooms and pink punch of the refreshment table primed for it. You could hear the hush in the room; you could hear how the need to bust out laughing had built up and built up, reaching its peak when Vincent Silvano Jr. walked on stage. We needed Vince to be a goof. He could have cemented his rep clear through high school.

Glen was there, by himself. I waved to him across the room. I was sad that we couldn't sit together, but the JVs were all around us, and Glen could not be added to that mix. He wore a blue shirt and a blue tie. He was smiling so hard his face must have hurt.

The indefatigable Mrs. Hunt was all day accompanist, and she looked at Vince, and Vince nodded, and she launched into the opening riff. Vince sang "The Rose of Tralee." He'd told me all about the song, and how he had wanted to do a Dorsey piece but they couldn't fit it into the theme, so Mrs. Hunt had dragged this number out, thinking because it was Irish and so were most of us, everyone would like it. It's funny the things you focus on. Mrs. Hunt's red dress had this big furry hem at the bottom, which I guess she thought gave the dress intriguing movement when she walked, but which bunched up there under the level of the piano bench like a great red python, and if you lost focus for a moment you almost thought, or hoped, it was a python, and that the music would be drowned out by Mrs. Hunt screaming and fighting for her life in the coils of the red constrictor. I was tangenting on Mrs. Hunt's dress because I was so afraid for Vince. It was clear it wasn't a goof, but maybe the guys would laugh anyway, and maybe I'd laugh with them. Maybe Vince would hear my voice laughing out of all the others.

Vince was wearing a white shirt and gray pants and a green tie with shamrocks on it, and behind him loomed a giant shamrock covered in shiny green wrapping paper, which stood for Ireland. I noticed everything because I was afraid to notice anything in particular. I feared not even being a god out of Olympus would get him through this. In the center section Glen was leaning forward in his seat, his palms turned up on the tops of his knees. He was as afraid as I.

When Vince began to sing, though, a strange thing happened. He wasn't funny. He wasn't funny or pathetic or sarcastic, or pleading-for-love, or any of the embarrassing things he might have been. Nor was he the sudden Caruso that would have been the other end of the continuum, campy in its own way, if a little more surprising. He was this earnest kid singing a pretty song, straight-backed and bright-eyed, as if he'd never had so much fun. We'd been giving all this thought to him, and he absolutely none to us, just out there singing his song. People didn't know what to do. I looked at the guys around me while one kind of smile faded from their lips, and another took its place. Someone did guffaw, but the guffaw was thin and uninspired, and didn't start the avalanche its maker hoped for. Vince warbled the last "The Rose of Tralee," bowed, and turned to walk off, then stopped for the applause, as though surprised that it happened for him the way it happened for everybody else. That was it. Samuella Lowe came on in a black geisha wig to do some Japanese cherry blossom number, and the show went on.

They gave out prizes at the end of the show for the best acts. Everybody was flabbergasted when the hoods doing the Apache dance to "Hawaiian War Chant" won first prize, because they really were the best, and we didn't expect our teachers to acknowledge it. They gave out prizes for courage, usually to kids who couldn't sing who tried to sing anyway, or who couldn't act and tried to act anyway. Vince didn't get any of the prizes, for being good or for being bad, and that was exactly right. No sentiment, no excuses, just the damn song, take it or leave it. I don't know about anybody else, but Glen and I were proud of him.

"The Rose of Tralee," by the way, is about a girl, and not about a flower at all.

A big crowd milled around in the lobby. Vince was surrounded by boys congratulating him with the uncertain tone of those who didn't know if they'd had one pulled over on them or not. The big lights over the school entranceway, which had been turned off so long because of air raid drills, were on now that the war was all but accomplished and because the talent show was a big deal in that remote age. Out of the wash of light, like a god from Olympus, strode Coach Vincent Silvano Sr., looking like a movie star, gigantic and out of place.

It would be hard to guess why Coach Silvano and his posse showed up at the middle school talent show. The high school and the middle school were on the same campus, and shared music and art teachers and the occasional assembly speaker, but the high school coaches were notoriously indifferent to anything from the middle school unless its voice had changed and it had hair on its balls. The possibility that he'd come because his son was in the show was so remote that no one we knew even considered it. Anyway, in that case he came two hours late. Coach was surrounded, as he always was, by bruisers from the varsity football team. You could see why they loved him. If not burlier than some of them, he was a big, strong man, one of those men who can appear stylish and put together while never tending visibly to wardrobe or to person. His black hair gleamed in the light of the school lobby. You felt his slouching and casually hoodlum air were deliberate foils to his movie star looks. The girls went on about his blue eyes, which he narrowed to look like a cowboy squinting into the sunset, or Bogart taking a drag on a cigarette. He was an impressive man. His beauty customarily wore a jacket of aggression. Coach needed to look good, but not too good. Pretty is not taken seriously, and if there was one thing the Coach was, it was taken seriously. He was an American man's man. I know that because my mother said so, with more enthusiasm than I wanted to detect. That most of his boys had crushes on him was assumed and never mentioned. It was something they'd grow out of, and, for a time, that emotion provided the fire behind his victorious teams. They were forever winning one for the Coach.

Coach and his boys lounged on one side of the lobby, balancing on one foot with the other braced flat against the wall, identical in every detail, indifferent to the exodus of the talent show audience with their chit-chat and their cooing of praise, and sometimes tittering of mockery. They managed to appear indifferent and watchful at once. Put uniforms on them and you might imagine yourself in a prison camp movie. Coach knew who I was, of course, but I gave up the idea of going over and saying hello. He was best looked at from afar.

Vince wanted to backtrack into the auditorium and disappear, but he had been spotted. One of the bruisers was pointing right at him, and whispering in Coach's ear. So on Vince came toward his father, his steps hesitating in a way clear to everyone but himself. When he was near enough, Coach reached out and flipped the end of Vince's shamrock tie.

"Nice," Coach said, the way a crocodile would say it.

The bruisers all laughed, a deep tittering, like girls dropping an octave in some unfamiliar atmosphere. Coach stared at his son in a way calculated to make him as comfortable as possible for as long as possible. Coach jerked his head toward the auditorium and said, "What the hell is this?"

Vince responded hopefully, "Did you hear me?"

"No I didn't hear. It's not about that. Do you mean to play for me next year?"

"Yes sir, if . . . I mean, if it's—"

Coach reared his hand back and delivered Vince a blow across the face. Everyone had stopped to watch the drama in the lobby, and most everyone gasped when the blow connected. Vince staggered back. His hand moved as if trying to comfort his face, but in the end stayed at his side. He stood up, to take another one if that's what Coach planned. No one dared speak. Except Glen Copland. Out of all that stunned silence came a little laugh, brief and pointed.

"Oh, big man," Glen said, smirking at Coach as though he'd caught him with his pants down.

Coach roared toward Glen with both fists up. He hissed under his breath, "You fucking homo. Are you the one who—"

"Maybe I am and maybe I'm not, but all you need to know is that if you touch me I'll have your job and anything you will ever own."

In a time when teachers beat kids all the time, it was hard to measure how much of the threat was serious and how much bravado, but there Glen was smirking with his chin against Coach's fist. Coach backed down. Coach whirled on his boy and said, "You ever embarrass me like that again and you won't be able to play football. A fucking talent show?" Coach spit the last two words out as if they were poison.

Coach Zeus and his entourage passed through the lobby doors to the sound of manufactured laughter, and out into the night. We all stood for a moment, dumbstruck. Finally Glen grinned and said, "And he didn't even hear you sing."

Vince spent that night with me. He didn't tell me what happened when he finally went home, and I didn't ask. It was the end of his entertainment career.

V

We got Calvin Cummings after we left Nancy McWhirter. I think it was a deliberate calculation on the part of the school, for Cummings was as by-the-book as McWhirter had been innovative. One of Coach Silvano's former stars come home, Cummings was as steely and inflexible as she had been gushy and accepting. It sounds like it would have been a shock; it wasn't, but rather like a family, where one parent fills roles the other doesn't, and like most families, it worked out pretty well. After initial nostalgia for McWhirter's softness and nurturing, we began to like Mr. Cummings and cherish his less lavishly doled-out affection. We liked his gruff voice and almost undetectable hesitancy of speech, a manly lisp, especially when he said childish words like "puppy" or "arithmetic." We liked his being sternly committed to his rules, however arbitrary. Without losing our crushes on Miss McWhirter, whom we often visited before class began, we were happy with Mr. Cummings, and adored him as, somewhere deep inside, a Marine must adore his drill sergeant. Vince adored him in particular, for he was a stern, strong man in whom there was no streak of cruelty. He was as Coach Silvano might have been.

He was also so handsome you lost track of what he was saying from time to time. Blond hair nearly shaved, fit slim body, severe wardrobe selections, he looked like a fighter pilot or an admiral one shore-leave. He'd mustered out of the Navy two weeks before he showed up in class. Larry Bibby leaned over in his seat the first day and whispered to Tilden, "Have you ever noticed how all Coach's favorites look like movie stars?" Larry let his wrist fall limp and put on this Daffy Duck lisp and added, "What's with that?" Tilden rolled his eyes and let it pass, but the comment stayed with me. I figured it explained something. More than one person asked why Coach never served in the war.

I'd been happy sitting in a front seat for a change—the name "Summers" usually put you back and to audience left of every damn classroom. I was so close I could smell Cummings' Old Spice. But one morning he motioned for our whole row to move a seat back. Before I had time to protest, he gave my seat to a new kid, a girl. Teacher's brief intro informed us that Sherry came to us from Alabama, from whence her father had been transferred, and we were to be ladies and gentlemen and welcome her into our family.

"Sherry, would you like to tell us something about yourself?"

Sherry stood, turned to the class without a trace of self-consciousness, and spoke in this molasses drawl that even we full-fledged Southerners found delicious. I've no idea what she said, though I was listening intently. Finally, I was grateful for Cummings putting her in front of me, where I could—nay, had to—watch the back of her head for a couple of hours a day. Her little-girl string of pearls fastened exactly in the middle of the back of her neck, and never seemed to deviate. I wondered how she managed that.

Sherry turned around in her seat to ask me questions from time to time. Normally Cummings would have come down on that hard, but it was her first day, and there were things she needed to know, and it made it unnecessary to stop class to fill her in. Besides, I think Cummings was a little sweet on her. Gentlemanly behavior was big with him, and a frail Alabama girl in a new environment offered all sorts of opportunities to the gentleman. I liked when she spoke to me. The brown-but-with-a-golden-light eyes and the deep-for-a-girl purr of her voice were exciting in ways I had never had to put into words before. After class Mr. Cummings barked over his shoulder, "Good work taking care of the new kid, Summers."

Something else was going on down there. I threw wood under my pants when she turned around to talk to me, or when she moved so the string of little pearls moved, or when I just happened to think about her. I wasn't used to this. Early on I put my hand on my hard dick to figure out what was happening and what I should do about it, but a ferocious glance from Cummings up front informed me that wasn't the right tactic. I don't know that I blamed Sherry. It seemed vaguer and more nebulous than that, as though the whole world reeked pheromones and I inhaled some with every breath.

We got older. Our bodies changed. Vince had been a little tubby as a kid. Now he was a panther. His dad was a panther, too; always had been. It's a shame they were at odds: they were practically the same person. Sherry was changing my attitude toward my own body. It had needs that were— this is difficult to explain—different from *my* needs. There were times when we would be at odds, the body and I. The curious thing was that ever since I'd seen Vince and Glen kissing, I assumed that buddy-love was a preliminary to boy-girl relations. I'm not saying it's *not*, ever, but it wasn't for me. I actively tried to feel enthused around Tilden or my buddies on the squad, and though I liked them and felt comfortable with them, what I'd seen on the camping trip was not liking or comfort. Vince manufactured reasons to be with Glen away from Tilden and me, so I assume it still went on. My latency was big, stupid, and lasted longer than almost anybody else's, but when I came out of it I was a full-fledged straight guy, mildly disappointed that I'd never gotten it on with one of my buddies.

Watching Vince on the football field was a lesson in the capabilities of the human body. Plenty of those meaty farm boys from the coves were bigger than him, but he was fast and mean. His impulses in a tight spot were nearly always right. He played smart. Had to, I guess, because he wasn't all that big. Andonian, the JV coach, got a good look at us all back in the seventh grade scrimmage, and I think he started grooming us for our destinies from that point. Vince was built like a quarterback. He moved like a quarterback. He looked like a quarterback. It was fate written in the stars.

I was his left tackle. I knew I was going to be Vince's left tackle before I even read the high school roster. It was the sort of thing a guy like me was destined to be: a guy like Vince's left guard. Like most QBs, Vince was right-handed, and I could protect his blind side when he reared back to pass down the field. I took the hits for him. I landed face down with my mouth full of turf while he danced in the end zone. It was all I wanted. And who was his right tackle? Of course it was Tilden Roundtree, tough, understated, yeoman-of-Sparta, never-a-stupid-mistake-making Tilden. It was good. It was perfect. Through the season, three of the four musketeers were together all day long.

By the time we left middle school, Vince was so handsome that the rest of us just gave up and accepted his dating leftovers. Melissa What's-her-name was his main squeeze for a while, then that girl who called herself Kitten. I forget everybody's name these days. But I can still see them, always the perkiest, always the prettiest. Teased hair. Angora. Little heart necklaces from their daddies on their sixteenth birthdays. They lined up at the locker room door. Except Sherry. I got her. When Vince saw I was mooning over Sherry he left her strictly alone.

We'd go double dating, or triple dating with Tilden and Mary Andonian, the JV coach's daughter. I was so proud. We were all so good-looking, so strong and healthy. It's like we were the queens and kings of Eddie Rickenbacker High School, wafting our cologne about us, flashing our white teeth. Tilden busted a finger once, but other than that we sailed through the football experience uplifted and unmarred. We were like America itself: good-looking, victorious in the moment, destined for victory in the time to come.

Glen didn't play sports. He was fast, and could have made the track team if he'd wanted to, but track didn't have all that much glamour back in the day, and anyhow, he showed no interest. He kept pretty much invisible in high school, one of those kids who wears a backpack and sits beside you in Algebra and you never know what's going on with them, and somehow never manage to ask. Debate team, I think, but there's no picture to confirm that in the yearbook. He was the one of our gang whose name people would forget. He was known as "Oh . . . the other one" as often as he was by his name. He didn't seem to care. He even called himself "the other one." This made Vinny grin one of his big movie star grins.

Every so often we renewed acquaintance with the Falls. We'd have a boys' night at one of the old camping spots, hauling our illicit booze and our dirty magazines up from the parking lot—instead of miles on foot through the forest, the way we did when we were kids. The swifts went away in the winter, so on winter junkets we didn't hang around much at the lip of the Falls, where it was blistering cold anyway. We'd huddle around the fire and crow about how wonderful it was to have the women off our backs for a weekend, how high maintenance they were and all that—though one noted we talked, at least for the first few hours, of very little else. We never opened the magazines. I guess the girly mags were there in case anyone came across us all cuddled up in the dead of night. Tits and ass would make that OK. In summer we did open the magazines, and masturbated like we heard they were going to put a tax on it. It's each boy's secret what he thinks about to make it happen. Glen wasn't dating yet, but he'd laugh whenever we'd make a joke about our girls; he'd listen closely when we needed to talk about them seriously. He was good company, the perfect confidant. Maybe his fling with Vince lay way in the past, Vince being such a hound-dog with the girls these days.

One evening Jake Hannerty sauntered by our camp. He was with the Church Street gang. There were six or seven of them, and we could hear them bellowing and carrying on through the acre of woods that lay between us. A prime weekend night, and all the guys in school were hunched over sloppy little fires with their buddies, complaining about girls—or lusting after the ones they didn't have—easing out of the tensions of the week. Hannerty had to take a piss or something, and when he walked past us we all waved and looked away, to let him have his privacy, but he stopped dead and said, "Copland?"

Glen said, "Hannerty!"

"Shit man," Jake said. "Don't you get enough of this place? I see you every time I come."

Jake made his way a decent distance into the woods. We could hear him pissing into soft pine needles. Maybe I was the only one to take heed of what he said. The expectation—tacit, unarticulated, but an expectation nevertheless—was that one would not come to the Falls alone. The surface reason was that it was dangerous. The more subtle reasons included the feeling that it was the setting for the deeds of the Brotherhood, and without the Brotherhood, nothing should happen at all. Maybe I heard wrong. Maybe Hannerty was bullshitting, the way one does.

I eyeballed Glen. He had that look on his face you have when you're hoping nobody paid attention to what was just said.

I couldn't help myself. Vince and Tilden were off doing something, and I took the occasion to say, "So, Glen, you've been coming up here yourself?"

"Sort of."

"Sort of?"

"Not for . . . not for anything like that."

Glen saw that I had no idea what "that" meant. He sighed. He opened his backpack and pulled out a canvas bag. It wasn't a bag, really, but a flat sheet of khaki canvas rolled around and around layers of something. Slowly he unrolled the bag. Inside, pressed flat between sheets of wax paper, and then rolled up like precious oil paintings, were fern leaves and liverworts and bright feathers fallen from birds Glen might have known but I did not.

"What do you call that?"

"Oh . . . specimens. I don't know."

Glen shrugged, but it was all right. He was a collector. A scientist. That was all right. It was firmly among the activities that would have been all right. I sighed in relief of a danger averted, without knowing exactly what the danger might be.

Tilden and Vince had been back in camp for about ten seconds when commotion arose in the temporarily over-populated woods. I thought they'd set fire to something or taken a crap on somebody's bedroll, but when the noise began—most of it seemed to come from the Church Street camp—they looked as bewildered as anybody. Jake Hannerty came sprinting back through the woods. He was tall and lanky, and looked like a giraffe loping on, pushing the pine boughs to one side or the other. The look on his face was not graceful.

"Hansen!" he managed to gasp out. "Hansen!"

Glen said, "Hansen? What do you mean? Timmy Hansen?"

Hannerty nodded frantically and continued flying through woods. We could hear him a way off crying "Hansen! Hansen!" at the next circle of sleeping bags.

It would have been nice if we hadn't known what he meant, but we did. Tilden jumped up and stamped out the fire. We all got ourselves arranged and lit out at a dead run for the brink of the Falls.

The upper reaches of the gorge came alive with boys climbing up and down crying "Timmy! Timmy!" If he'd answered, I don't know how he would have been heard in the din, but adrenaline was so high it was not the time to try to talk it down. This kid we all knew, Marky . . . Marky something, sat on a stone with his feet in the water. When we first came out of the trees, his face hid in his hands, but he lifted it up in a second and screamed. His face was red and swollen. You had to pay close attention to make out what he was screaming. It was: "I DON'T KNOW WHAT THE FUCK HAPPENED! HE WAS RIGHT THERE! HE WAS JUST FUCKING RIGHT THERE!"

His face would fall back into his hands, and a couple of the Church Street boys would pat him and coo to him that it was all right. Everybody knew it wasn't. It wasn't all right. In a minute the scarlet swollen face, streaming tears, reared up again, howling: "I DON'T KNOW WHAT THE FUCK HAPPENED! HE WAS RIGHT THERE! HE WAS JUST FUCKING RIGHT THERE!"

Easy to read. Marky and Timmy had been horsing around at the rim of the Falls, showing off for one another. Marky looked down to swat a deerfly on his leg, and when he looked up, Timmy Hansen was gone. It was that simple. The Falls got at least one every generation. That was the lore. That was the truth as we told it. No one would admit to heaving a sigh of relief that the sacrifice for our generation was now known and accomplished.

We kept climbing around and screaming, but we all pretty much knew what would be found in the plunge pool at the bottom of the falls. Someone jumped into a car and headed for town. About an hour into the drama, the police showed up. Chief Dadlez had come up from Asheville to helm the village force right at the New Year, and so far he had been all about garnering good will, helpful and cheerful and spruce, getting kittens out of drain pipes, that sort of thing. I didn't see him when he arrived at the gorge rim, but

Vince said it took him a while to get oriented and organize a party to find the body. We were ahead of him there.

I knew the trails and footholds pretty well, so I managed to get to the floor of the gorge, all the way down. The spray of the falls cooled my sweat. I could hear boys hollering over the roar of the water; none seemed to have gotten down this far. I hoped they'd stop trying, so nobody else would fall. I slipped my way over the slick rocks toward the plunge pool. Rainbows stood in concentric arches over the green moss and the blinding white stone. Seagulls wheeled and soared as though the din were surf and not a plunging river. I stopped myself from noticing how beautiful everything was. It was not the time. Down by the pool one discerned two shapes. One was horizontal, a body, shedding red plumes into the relatively calm pool it had drifted into. The other was vertical, standing by the water: Glen Copland. The light hit his Boy Scout knapsack covered with patches so it looked like a tropical bird had landed on his shoulders.

The force of waters buffeted Timmy's body slowly to shore. Glen waited for it. When he was close enough, Glen knelt and pulled Timmy in by his baggy denim cuff. I know I could have run and helped, but I sensed something sacred going on, that I should stay out of it until I got the signal. So I watched as Glen hauled the poor broken boy out of the water. Timmy was bigger than Glen, so it wasn't easy, but Glen got him out onto the encircling shingle of round stones. Glen didn't know what to do now any more than I would have, so he knelt down and took Timmy in his arms, to keep him warm until help came. I walked to their side then. I didn't know what to do except to hold Glen as Glen held Timmy. At last, the firemen came with ropes and a canvas stretcher. Dadlez held them up for some regulation or other, but when he finally set them loose, the firemen, who were town boys too, muscled down the same paths and footholds we all knew.

It had been a while since the Falls had taken anybody. The town had forgotten how to deal with it. People looked at each other in the streets with the look that said, "What are we supposed to do?" They put Timmy's face on a poster and stapled it up in the grocery stores and on the church bulletin boards. They were up a long time, the posters were, until they faded too much and someone took them down. He was a good kid. Everybody liked him. We all knew the Hansen family. It was just awful. Nobody admitted to thankfulness that there remained three sisters and two other brothers in the family. The numbers of the remnant didn't make it any better, but they kept it from being worse.

Chief Dadlez reacted to the tragedy by closing the park. This was futile on many levels. For one thing, you could close the park (which was a parking lot and a few picnic tables) without limiting access to the Falls very much. Most of us came up through the woods paths anyway. The cove boys used the imposing metal "Keep Out By Police Order" signs for target practice. They made a lovely *ting* when hit with birdshot. But Dadlez had a hard-on about this. He kept throwing people in jail for being at the Falls, until the county prosecutors told him to stop because they weren't going to prosecute. They made him take the barricades away, it being state property and not the chief's private domain. We understood, though. We never wanted to go through that again either. Had Dadlez been local he would have understood that safety is achieved not by barricades, but by brother looking after brother. Marky was a mess for months, not because anyone blamed him (they didn't) but because he was supposed to look out for Timmy, and for the briefest and most excusable instant, he had not.

The chief did have thick blue lines painted at the cliffs' edge, to tell people how close it was safe to come. Nobody begrudged him that. He ordered the lines repainted and repainted until long after people—except the people who were there—had forgotten who Timmy Hansen was.

It was a time when parents would never ask "Where are you going?" for there was almost no conceivable trouble one could get into in our little town. They asked then, for a while. "Where are you going?" they'd hiss, as if tigers and rapists lurked just outside the door. You learned never to answer, "To the Falls." What was the use in upsetting them? The Falls would have whom it wanted. They would call you if you didn't come on your own. Furthermore, if the Falls claimed one every generation, Timmy Hansen had made us safe until we had sons of our own.

VI

Vince raised the town out of depression. Didn't take that long. Football practice started in August, and by the time a hint of frost hung in the air again Coach sensed that, through his son's leadership as quarterback, Eddie Rickenbacker High had a chance at the 2A playoffs for the first time since he himself captained the team. We took the Conference. The well-heeled downstate schools obliged us by picking one another off while we nibbled away in the far west, eking through some matches, annihilating our opponents in others. Reporters came from Raleigh and Charlotte and took our photos—Vince's photo, actually, though sometimes we were gathered 'round as supporting cast. Game followed game, and when one ended in victory, kids in red and gold streamed down from the stands to lift us on their shoulders. Even Vince, who'd expected his life to turn out in something like this way, seemed taken aback. A clipping service sent him articles about himself from papers way downstate. He showed me when they mentioned me, as they, once or twice, did.

We lost in the sudden-death second round to some low-foreheaded glandular cases from Durham. Coach said they won because they were used to living around colored kids and fighting their way through the halls every day. What did we know? There were two black families in town, and where their kids went to school I had honestly no idea. It wasn't Eddie Rickenbacker.

Coach hung publicity photos of the Durham squad in the locker room, so we could build up hatred toward them for the next match-up. They were mostly seniors and we'd never see those individuals again, but the sentiment mattered. We wanted to smash them into the ground and run our cleats over their broken spines. Nobody had heard them call us hillbillies, but we assumed they had, and were therefore determined to make that epithet one of fear and respect.

If I look at my old report cards, I see that I took chemistry and English and history and some pretty interesting stuff, but I almost literally have no memories of my junior year but Sherry and football. And by "football" I mean Vince and Tilden and the guys and the cheerleaders, all the sweat and bruises, and, when autumn came, the cries of victory. Dear God, I was in shape. I look at pictures of myself then and wonder if we were the same person.

No man is an entire team, but Vince came close as anyone could. His passes arced to his receivers like babies to their mothers' arms. He ran the ball like a goddamn gazelle. He leapt over tackles as if they were lying down. When he got into the end zone he stopped and gazed kind of stupidly at the ball as if he were not quite sure he had made the touchdown, waiting for the voice of the crowd for confirmation. I've never seen anyone like him, before or since. We were golden, all of us that year, but Vince was diamond and uranium. Coach beamed at him even when nobody was looking. Walking down the hall at school was a march of triumph. I wonder sometimes if Sherry would have married me without the glamour of that season around my head. I'm too prudent to ask. I got voted Outstanding Left Tackle by the sportswriters of North Carolina. I have the certificate framed in my den. Vince collected so many certificates, so many trophies he stopped setting them out on his mother's shelves. The newspaper ran a feature on how many articles they had run on him in the previous eighteen months, and it turned out to be more than the mayor. You could watch people just standing back and looking at him in the streets. The border mountains had never produced anything like him. Having Vince as my best friend seemed such a stroke of fortune that I would probably never ask anything else of the world.

It was that summer, the one between the first two championship years, that Glen went to Scout Camp out west. His life thus became temporarily more interesting than ours. Vince would gather us together and read letters Glen had written from his bunk under the Grand Tetons, or wherever the hell it was. Vince read the letters aloud, and when he did he made the salutation "Dear Vince and Arden and Tilden," though you could see by the mark of the letters through the page that all Glen had written was "Dear Vince":

> Philmont is great, for the most part. JC, the guy who teaches rock climbing, is cool, and I'm getting good at it. The cliffs used to look a lot taller than they do now. Can't wait to show you my bruises and sunburn, and even a snakebite, from something harmless, though, so the bragging rights aren't so great. You have to shake your boots in the morning to make sure there aren't scorpions curled up inside. I wouldn't want to live in my boots, but there's no accounting. Never ate so much in my life. When you're climbing cliffs and riding horses all day, you build up an appetite.

Dad's almost forgiven me for trying to get out of coming here this summer. I told him I wanted to spend the summer with you, but he didn't even understand what I meant. Or maybe he did. I do like the Scouts, though, and I'm learning so much. You and Tilden and Arden are all the time showing me up in the woods. This is catch-up, sucker! Dad spent a lot of money and went to a lot of trouble, blah blah blah, so I make sure to tell him what good things we're doing and how I'm really getting use out of his money. I am having a good time and all that, but I'm not glad I came. I miss you. I miss you like hell. Thank you for that last night together. I carry the feel, the touch, the sound of your voice with me everywhere. I'll see you in twenty-six days.

Love, Glen

Tilden said, "What's that touch and sound of your voice stuff?"

"Oh, he's bullshitting. You know how we're always bullshitting." But Vince's face was bright red. He hadn't edited the letter first. He kept reading the letters as they arrived afterward, but you could tell by the way he moved his head that he wasn't reading all of them like they were written.

One day in Youth Sunday School we had a visitor, a whippet-thin gent who had been a missionary in China, and sort of looked Chinese now, with a wispy beard and long eyes and a wise bald head. He was about a thousand years old. He'd taught the Chinese to grow better wheat, or something. We were talking about the things you talk about with a thousand-year-old missionary, when Doug Lazorn—ever the wise-ass—made the point that heaven must be boring after a while, since even the best thing drawn out to eternity is boring. The old guy smiled. He said we—or at least

Doug—had gotten it wrong. You should think of paradise not as an infinite extension of moments, but one moment of perfect bliss in which you live fully, in the moment, of the moment, without thought for what came before or would come after. Before the end of the day I started applying this to my life, which was so good at the moment that I made a deliberate effort not to think of whatever might come after. Kids not in bliss might be picking out colleges and writing admissions essays. Not us. We were in the clouds and not ready to step down. Maybe we can be forgiven for thinking our lives would never change, that all was perfect and a gold haze lay on the encircling mountains. We were OK, I think; even our arrogance was a kind of gratitude.

VII

I remember the day and hour that Andy came home for good. He ordered us not to bother picking him up at the station in Asheville. He said he'd get a ride with one of his buddies, so the first we saw of him was when Clarence, his best friend from high school, braked in our driveway and helped Andy out of the back seat of his jalopy. Clarence had been a Marine, and the back of the jalopy was painted with something that looked like an amoeba (it was meant to be The World), under which was stenciled in flame-red letters, *Semper Fidelis*. Andy was still a little weak, and it gave me joy to take over from Clarence and help him into the house, and hence into our room where he would sleep for a couple of days before we could start the long-planned-for welcome home party. The way he was lying in his bed I could see the bandage over his wound. I lifted up his shirt a little so I could see better. The place was smaller now than it had been in the photos. If I could judge by the bandage, the entry hole was no larger than a quarter. Got his lung, though, and a couple of other things inside there, and sent him home to us.

Andy would have been halfway through college if he hadn't gone to war, but he seemed older. His body was hard and compact. I remembered him bigger than he was, but I realized he had not shrunk; I had grown. Something in the way the bullet had entered him made him prone to muscle spasms, and sometimes his whole chest would seize up, and he had to breathe real shallow to breathe at all, and sweat would be pouring off him because of the pain. He smiled at you then to let you know it would pass and you shouldn't worry. You could get him a glass of water. That made it better. He was not doing anything different than he had done before, I guess, but he was doing it in a different way. It was hard to put your finger on. Andy was sad. Had he killed a lot of people? I'd let him settle in before I started peppering him with questions.

Mom said, "He's going to be spending a little time with us while he decides what to do." That was fine with me. I thought he and I would take over Dad's hardware store in the fullness of time, Summers Family Feed and Hardware, but that didn't seem to be his dream anymore. Well, I'd do it, and hold his place until he was ready.

My brother's friend, Clarence, had been part of the undifferentiated cloud of young male energy that was my brother's friends, not particularly noticed or marked. My brother's friends were kind to me—I gathered from other kids that this was not a universal state of affairs—and Clarence the kindest, even, once in a while, staying to play with me if he came over and Andy wasn't home. Clarence was the one on whom my mother pressed an extra apple or one more pass of the cookie plate. She did this with Andy within the family, too, in a gesture I recognized from the first was not really favoritism. Andy got an extra kiss on the head when we were leaving in the morning. If there was an extra slice of chocolate pie, Andy was offered it, because everybody knew it was his favorite, and how he'd eat away the meringue, because he didn't like that so much, and leave himself just a sagging edge of shimmering chocolate for the end. Andy and Clarence were not greedy or favored: they were sad, and all the more so because for the sadness there was no adequate explanation. Mom was just trying to bring light where the shadow lay deepest.

Clarence was the first person not in my gang whom I noticed at the Falls. One of his northern relatives gave Vince a pair of second-hand snowshoes in time for one of the few days they could have been used. Snow fell in great sloppy clumps, as though the Southern sky, unused to the exercise, didn't know quite how properly to snow. The river was not itself frozen, but its spray froze wherever it hit the cold rock. The upper gorge was a roofless hall of blue ice. The Falls was thwarted by ice in some of its customary streams, and shot out from the cliffs at unexpected angles. Vince forged ahead on his second-hand snowshoes while Tilden and I ran behind with the great loping strides you need in snow. It was great exercise. We poured sweat which froze on our mufflers to a salty white rime. I was falling back a little—it didn't matter, because they would have to come back the same way if they were going to get out of the forest—and leaned over with my hands on my knees to pant the breath back into me. From that new angle I could see a thin wisp of smoke near the edge of the forest, and a flicker of pale gold under it.

I jogged over and found Clarence sitting alone beside the pathetic campfire. This struck me as strange, for Andy's friends were as adhesive as mine, and the only one you ever saw alone in the old days was Andy himself, and that mostly when he was on his bike delivering the *Times* before the break of day. One of the rules of the Falls, passed down from generation to generation, was that one should not go alone. To go alone was asking for it. Whatever haunted the Falls was better faced by two or three than by one. Clarence looked different when not diluted by the boy swarm. He was compact and muscular, almost an adult, with the curly reddish hair of his family. Handsome, I thought, while he was still an unknown boy beside an incidental fire. When I recognized him, this thought faded, and he became just Clarence.

He was in similar confusion. He stared at me for a moment before he knew where he knew me. "Ardo," he said, using my brother's nickname for me. I decided I would let him.

Clarence stood up. He removed his glove and placed his hand flat on the top of my head, like a priest giving a blessing. He said, "I wondered when this was going to happen."

"What?"

"You and the other pipsqueaks finding the Falls."

"It happened a while back. I'm surprised Andy didn't—"

"Oh, I haven't been hanging out with the gang as much as I used to."

Clarence had been drinking. I was a bit of a prig, so I filed this away for later accusation. He was dirty, too. He had been out on the rim of the gorge for more than a few hours.

"You the first of your group? I bet it was Coach's kid. Vince."

"No, it was me."

"Good work. Your brother was first too."

Clarence gazed over my head at something. I resisted the urge to turn and look too. I guessed it was just the snow careering into what was already the velvet dark of the deep forest.

"Me, I was so happy. So proud when Andy brought us here. I took to it most," Clarence said. "I was looking for it, in a way, without knowing what 'it' was. Now I can't seem to stay away. Lost a girlfriend over it already. She gave me a . . . what do you call it?"

"Ultimatum?"

"She gave me an ultimatum. Stop coming here . . . spend more time with her . . ." Clarence stopped. Perhaps he realized that wasn't exactly a full-formed ultimatum. He belched nobly.

"You know, I should have thought about bringing some substantial food out here."

"I'm sorry, we didn't . . . I mean, Vince got these snowshoes he wanted to try out—"

"No, no, it's OK. Shouldn't have come out here. Not alone. It's one of Andy's rules. He's very serious about those rules. How the hell's he doing anyway?"

"Fine. He's waiting for you to visit."

"Oh, I will. I brought him home, you know."

"I know. I was there."

"I want to get myself cleaned up a little . . . before I . . . You know how he worries about the people close to him. I don't want him . . . to . . ." Clarence seemed to lose his train of thought. He looked at his sad little camp and said, "I guess I didn't know where else to go." He gestured toward the efficient little plume of his fire. "Fire's nice though. Marines taught me that. Come over and warm yourself if you like."

To please my brother's friend I went and held my hands over his fire. It did feel nice. It was cold on the ridge, and night was coming.

"You could come back with us."

"Naw . . . I been drinking a little. Wouldn't do to go home drunk. Gotta work it off a little."

"It'll be dark—"

"All right with me. I like the dark. Andy and Louie, they'd have to scurry home at twilight . . . back in the day . . . maybe their moms were waiting . . . you'd know about that. But I'd stay out until the moon rose and I could see enough to find the trail. The moon doesn't always shine in other places, but there is always a moon here. I couldn't figure that out. I still think about it. 'The Place Where the Moon is Always Shining.' Must be what 'Wyona' means in Indian. If it weren't covered by the snow clouds, you'd see a moon now. Back in town it might just disappear. I don't know."

He reached into his backpack for a drink. Remembering me, he aborted the gesture, but not before I heard bottles clink together inside.

He put his forefinger to his lips in a shushing gesture. "Don't tell Andy, OK?"

"No."

"Don't tell anyone."

He was crying, or maybe he had caught some of the smoke from the campfire in his face. He inspected the dent his body had made in the snow—fragile and tiny in the face of the coming night—and said, "Jesus."

Then he said, "He's just like me."

"Who is?"

He motioned toward the path the snowshoes had made into the woods.

"Vince?"

"No, not Vince. His friend. His—well, you know."

"Tilden?"

"Not fucking Tilden. The one . . . the other one . . ."

"Glen?"

"Yeah, Glen."

"What do you mean?"

"He's here all the time by himself. I come and think I'll be alone, and catch a glimpse of him crawling around in the rocks. Looking at things."

"Him and his nature."

"Yeah. Makes me wish I had something like that. I had—" Clarence stopped and knitted his brow, trying to remember what it was he had. The effort proved too much. He bent over, laughing helplessly. When he almost had control of himself again, he wheezed out, "I can't . . . fucking . . . remember . . . what I had." He thought it was so funny. I did too, for his sake.

I saw Tilden and Vince reappear out of the forest. I wanted to say goodbye to Clarence, but he was still laughing, bent over with his hands on his knees, in exactly the stance I used a few minutes ago for exhaustion. I punched his arm. He nodded and waved me on, unable to cut the laughter long enough to say goodbye.

A storm came up that night and continued for two more nights, snow and snow and then blown and drifting snow. It would have been perfect for snowshoeing, but they were school nights, and by the time the weekend came the temperature was in the sixties and the snow was gone. Additionally, I got another invitation. Sherry decided we should use the winter thaw in some unexpected way. We should go on a January picnic.

Mrs. Tanseer packed Sherry and me a lunch and we cycled up 414 to the Falls. Sherry carried the lunches in her backpack, because she was less likely to act like a retard and take a spill, and we didn't need for all the sandwiches to be smashed when we got there. The day felt warm and the very unseasonableness of it assured us some privacy. Unmelted snow flashed in the shade of the trees. One sunny side of one rock on the bike path wore a blue spray of anemones. They had likely been blooming already, under the snow. I admired that. I admired that they would not bend to circumstance.

We'd eaten our lunches and stretched out on a sun-struck stone, a chip a glacier had broken off from another mountain a thousand miles to the north. We intended to take a nap in the sunlight, but we were too excited from the ride and the proximity of one another. Sherry sat so the light came through her hair into my eyes. I always thought of her hair as dark, not black, but black's cousin. With light in it like that, it went up in rays of red and dark gold, the dark of it like a shadow rather than a real color. The sun came too bright from that direction for me to see much else. I realized that, facing away from the sun the way she was, every detail of my face would be clear and illuminated. I lay exactly as a photographer would put me to take my picture in that light. I hoped she liked what she saw. I lay so the muscle of my arm made a bulge when I rested my head against it. She'd taken a liking to fashion, that you could get from the magazines at the hairdressers', and was giving me a run-down of designers I had never heard of and whose designs I could not imagine even with her detailed descriptions. I was clueless and I didn't mind. I was listening to her, not to the words. I vibrated with an electrical excitement that was partially agitation from the bike ride, partially something else I could not quite define. I was new to such matters, and it took me a while to recognize what I felt. This is it, I thought. For the first time I was certain what I wanted, and it was Sherry, and there would be no finesse, no delicacy up there in the wind and rock.

While she was still talking I leaned over and kissed her at the nearest part, which was her ankle. She stopped talking. She reached down and touched the spot I'd kissed. The light shone so bright in my face that I couldn't see her expression, but she hadn't slugged me, so I took the next step. I rose up on my knees so my mouth could find her face. She met me halfway. She met me more than halfway. I thought she was going to push me off the stone. We jumped at each other like a pair of cougars. I thought she was going to break my ribs, and then I thought I was going to break hers. I don't know exactly what thing led to the next, but in moments we were kissing, hard, hungrily, Sherry making little moans that turned me on all the harder. I'd never heard that. In all the kissing scenes in the movies, I had never heard moaning. I guess everyone conspires to save that for the real thing. Sherry smelled like grass and sun and the stone we had been lying on. She was under my shirt, chewing away, so I must have smelled all right.

Discretion did cross our minds. We slid down the far side of the stone, so we could not be seen from the path, or at all unless somebody climbed the boulder directly over our heads. The downside was that this gave us less than four feet of mossy shelf before the plunge into the gorge. This made our lovemaking compact and concentrated, and I can't say that was a detriment. Either Sherry had done this before, or girls were naturals at it in a way boys weren't. Whenever I fumbled she set me right; whenever I wondered what next to do, her hands and lips put forward a suggestion. I tried to pull away before I burst in her mouth, but that's what she wanted, and she wouldn't let me pull away, and I let go with a scream that amazes me in recollection. It echoed against the rocks of the gorge. It sounded like someone falling. When the waves had passed, she eased herself forward and lay down on top of me. We lay that way for a long time. My legs went to sleep under her, but I didn't care. Her hair flew around us and I could see nothing but that. I could feel a deep sigh in her that had no sound to it. She rolled onto the mossy stone beside us and sat up.

I said, "Oh boy."

This made her laugh. She leaned over with her chest over her knees and belted it out until tears came into her eyes. I loved the way Sherry laughed. It was anarchy personified. Now she was full in the light so I could see her. Her hair was dark again, waving around her head so that her laughter-tear-streaming brown-gold eyes were only sometimes visible. I couldn't believe how beautiful she was. I couldn't believe that someone that beautiful had accepted me—no, had chosen me. Sherry was leaning pretty close to the edge of the shelf now. Her laughter simmered down. But she didn't draw back. Something caught her eye. She focused on something in the gorge. The gorge and the bottom of the Falls were not visible from the rocks above, but some of it was from this new vantage, where none of us had been before. Neither Sherry nor I was uncomfortable with heights, so I got on my hands and knees and joined her at the brink.

"What are you looking at?"

She pointed. "Isn't it disgusting," she said, "how people are so careless—"

A white mass lay on a stone at the bottom, garbage that had dived over the falls, or perhaps been tossed by piggish picnickers. But it was on a dry slab of rock and too far from the Falls, so it became clear that whatever it was had been tossed deliberately, probably from the very spot where we lay.

We had both realized what we were seeing before either of us spoke again. Sherry said, "Fuck," in that way she had, at once pointed and contemplative. It was not garbage. It was a body. The little flapping motions we thought was paper flying around was the tail of a white shirt. Both the shirt and the stone were clearly stained red. We jumped on our bikes and rode in absolute silence back to town, at speeds around those mountain corners that only the urgency of our mission allowed. I knew even before we ran into the sheriff's deputies at Roscoe's Diner at the edge of town that it was Clarence.

I was curled up in bed when Andy got home, too excited to sleep, being a sort of hero, being one of those who had found the body. I didn't know what to say to my brother, so I pretended to be asleep. Andy came in and took off his jacket. The leather smelled of Andy, and it comforted me, as it always did. He dropped his clothes on the floor and kicked them under the bed to be sorted out in the morning. I heard his familiar sounds in the bathroom. He brushed his teeth. He entered the room and closed the door behind him. He didn't lie down. I knew he was standing in the middle of the room, listening to see if I were asleep. Then in a voice that sounded like it was coming from far away, I heard him say, "Buddy . . . buddy . . . what have you done?" Andy sobbed himself to sleep. The sound was loud enough that I don't think he heard me sobbing too.

I wakened to Andy brushing my hair back from my face. His face was puffy, his eyes sleepless. I supposed it was morning, though it was bitterly dark.

"Get up, Ardo. By the time you get your clothes on, it will be light enough."

I heard Andy on the phone downstairs as I dressed. He whispered, but it's surprising how the *s*'s of whispering carry. When I went down he stood on the porch, his bike and mine resting against the porch wall. Louie and Marcus were in the yard waiting. Louie and Marcus were all of his gang that were, for one reason or another, home from the war. Marcus was black and the Army didn't want him so much. Louie had asthma and flat feet. Marcus sucked on a gigantic thermos of coffee. The sweet smell of it filled the yard.

Andy said, "Saddle up, men. We ride."

I didn't know where we were going until Andy veered onto 414. We were going to the Falls. There were the sounds of legs pumping and lungs breathing around me, the sharp smells of the mountain morning. It would have been cold if we were not going fifteen miles an hour straight uphill.

Up ahead I could hear part of a conversation between Andy and Louie. Andy's buddies had come because he summoned them, not because they had any idea what was going on. I lost the front part, but the back part of what Andy said was, "—didn't do it to himself."

"It was an accident," Louie said, halfway between a question and a declaration.

"That's right."

"We're going to prove that?"

"That's right."

In the day since the news got out, people seemed more concerned over whether it was a suicide than the fact that Clarence was dead. He survived the war but didn't survive the peace. People didn't like that. People didn't want to know about that. People die, but when people die on purpose, especially the kind they like to say "have their whole lives ahead of them," people worry that something is wrong at the core of things. Rot at the root. Andy worried about that. He did not want for something to be wrong at the center of his friend's life. I knew now he had lain awake all night, thinking of this, measuring what he knew of his friend against the dark concept "suicide," deciding there was no resonance between them.

I'd never gotten to the Falls so fast. Not many cars could have gotten there much quicker. My lungs were bursting, but it felt great. All the guys stood by their bikes for a moment in the parking lot, blowing mist out of their mouths, catching their breaths, clouds of steam rolling off their bodies as if they were hot metal. Louie had his Atlanta Braves ball cap turned backwards on his head, which meant he was ready for action.

Louie said, "I say we split up and—"

I interrupted, "He had a camp here. A kind of . . . bivouac."

Andy looked at me. "That true? You know where it was?"

I nodded. I led them to the place where I'd found Clarence drunk five days before. A thin wisp of smoke, hardly discernible from the fog all around, still issued from the center ashes of his little fire.

Marcus said, "Clarence could build a fire on an iceberg and keep it burning in a hurricane."

We began to ransack the camp, gently, though, so no clue, no bit of proof, no salvageable memento could be lost. Andy found ropes and crampons. Marcus found a store of victuals, hoisted up into a tree against the bears, meant to last for at least a weekend.

Marcus said, "People intending to kill themselves do not bring Chef Boy-Ar-Dee."

Louie looked into Clarence's backpack. Inside were some clean clothes, and a pen, and a journal to write in with the pen.

"He kept a diary."

Andy said, "Close it up. We'll decide what to do later."

When we'd gathered what there was to gather, I made a suggestion.

"I think I know where he fell from. Sherry and I didn't just . . . come across him. We found him at a particular place."

I felt many pairs of eyes on me. When I looked up, Marcus grinned a big shit-eating grin. He said, "You two were making out, weren't you?"

Like a real man, I said nothing.

I brought them to our flat rock, which was not sunny now, but clammy and uninviting. I showed them how to drop over the far side and still have enough room to stand before the plunge to the abyss. The Falls roared so around us every word had to be blasted at the top of lungs. You had to lower yourself down from the ledge a little in order to see anything. Andy twisted tufts of grass in his grip trying to peer into the depths. Louie and Marcus held onto his legs.

"Fucking fog."

We'd never been to the Falls very early in the morning— and when we spent the night, we had not roused ourselves in time—and so didn't know when the fog finally burned away. Andy couldn't wait. He kept inching over the brink, Louie and Marcus holding onto him for dear life. Finally Andy's hand shot out like a thrown spear. He shouted, "There!"

We couldn't see, but we trusted he'd found something. Andy refused to move, lest it be an apparition and vanish when he did. When the fog blew thinner, we all peered over very carefully and saw what Andy saw. It was a length of rope, one frayed end caught in a fissure and the other descending we knew not where into the misty depths. As Louie was finding a spot to look over himself, his hand touched cold metal. It was a climber's anchor, a new one, that Clarence had clearly driven into the ground the day before to anchor his descent into the gorge. The drama came suddenly clear.

His rope broke.

His rope broke.

His rope broke. Maybe sheared on the knife edge of the black-and-white obsidian just under the overhanging brink. Andy began to cry. Everybody turned their heads into the fog where their expressions could not be seen. It had been an accident. The frayed rope on the stone wall shouted mercy.

Marcus said, "The Falls has claimed its own. Again."

As if Marcus's words had somehow broadcast through the fog and reached every ear in town, the streets and cafés and beauty parlors murmured with the sentence, "The Falls has claimed its own." Isolated people—and despite the radio and pretty good roads, we were hillbillies clinging to the cracked and crumbling side of the oldest mountain in the world—latch on to phrases and catch words as though they were some comfort, as though they were the truth. We latched on to "The Falls has claimed its own." I didn't know what it meant, beyond something someone might say almost automatically in a situation like that, something to give a random occurrence meaning, even a sinister one. I didn't know that it meant anything at all.

We'd made a tactical mistake that morning when we set out to vindicate Clarence. We'd left the beds of four young men empty at the break of day, young men known to be particular friends of the dead boy, young men known in general to be loyal and excitable. Young men have from time to time taken suicide as a team sport. On our bicycles we were too far away to hear the cry that went up from bedrooms and breakfast tables. We didn't hear the conversations over the telephone wires, nor partake in the shared vision of us crumpled together on the oozy rocks of Wyona Gorge. We didn't understand when several cars, speeding up 414 in the direction of the Falls, zoomed past us, broke with a squeal of tires, ground their engines trying to get turned around back our way on the narrow road. Why were they honking their horns? When we reached the town square—with horns and flashing high beams behind us—the paved space was overrun with cars, all our parents, all the neighbors of our parents. When we rolled into view heads turned like grasses in the wind, and we knew we were both welcome and in a peck of trouble.

Parents rushed toward us, not necessarily even our own. We were too bad to hug, too big to spank, so the street filled with parents and sons standing two feet from each other, bending forward but unable to touch, unable quite to figure out what the other was agitated about. Marcus' mother had her hand raised in the air, praising the Lord, or perhaps just barely stopping herself from bringing it down across the side of her son's head. Mom in her green housecoat, blowing steam through her lips with every word said, "Well, at least Andy was with you. I wouldn't have worried so much had I known that."

Chief Dadlez loitered at the edge of the crowd, taking it in. Andy broke away from Mom and began to bulldoze his way toward the chief. I tagged along behind. When Andy got about three inches from the chief's face, he said,

"You didn't even look."

"What do you mean?" said the chief, raising one brow a little, the way he did.

"You assumed Clarence killed himself, so you didn't even look."

"Now, Andy, I don't think this is the time or the place to—"

If the chief just hadn't had that patronizing smirk on his face, I think Andy would have shut up. If he'd just looked for a second like he was going to listen. The chief was so anxious to keep control that he let himself make a big mistake. He smirked at a man who had just seen where his best friend died.

"There's a spike driven in the rock . . . oh, we can show you where it is. If you're interested. Under the spike there's a length of broken rope. Right there in the rock. He fell. The rope broke. He fell."

Andy turned to the center of the milling crowd and repeated the words, loudly, slowly, clearly, "Clarence FELL. WE FOUND THE BROKEN ROPE. HE HAD CHEF BOY-AR-DEE. YOU DON'T BRING CHEF BOY-AR-DEE TO A SUICIDE. HE FELL. IT WAS AN ACCIDENT. ANYBODY WITH A BRAIN COULD SEE THAT."

I think Andy had more to say, but his voice choked with emotion. Andy had slapped me across the back of the head a couple of times when I was a nuisance, but I'd never seen him angry. He was angry then. He was so angry his voice would not come out right. He was so angry tears squeezed out the bottom of his eyes like drops from a twisted cloth. Dad moved over to him. Dad stood between him and the chief so if Andy's fury funneled down into throwing a punch at Chief Dadlez, he would be there to stop it.

Dadlez was a good man. He was generally up to the small challenges our town threw at him. He brought drunks safely home, negotiated truces between stores and teenaged shoplifters, rooted crazy old loonies out of their shacks in the coves without firing a shot. Part of the job was to have an opinion about everyone who might cross his path, and his opinion about Clarence was that he was a lost soul. The boys who protected him, his clutch of friends, would leave one day, would go to college or have families, and he would be lost still. Of course he would kill himself, either now, foreseeing it, or when the full despair of his lostness finally dawned on him. Watching the firemen drag his body out of the gorge, Dadlez had come to the conclusion that he had thrown himself there. Like Andy had said, he didn't look at anything else. Whether he was sorry or not was less important than retaining authority before his constituency. The smirk never left his face.

I think Andy intended to punch the son of a bitch until Dad came up out of the crowd like a big bass from under his stump in the river. Dad turned his back on Dadlez and pulled Andy, and then me, against his chest. Then he motioned to Marcus and Louie, bringing them over and crushing them against himself—and us—in an indiscriminate manner, as though he were the father of the whole world. He said, "Let's go home."

Dadlez said, "I don't think anybody is going anywhere until I get the details of what your boy just said. You don't contradict an official police report and then waltz right off without—"

We waltzed right off even as the chief was forbidding it. Dadlez didn't deserve that, but it felt so good.

Andy was shaken and exhausted when we got home. Mom would have, in times past, put him to bed, but I did it this time, Dad and me in the room settling him down and waiting for him to go to sleep. It seemed a man's thing, a thing of war and valor. When Andy eased into dreamland, I called Sherry to tell her the whole story. It would not be finished until I told her. I could see Mom smiling from the kitchen while we talked. I turned to face the wall so Mom wouldn't see the hard-on Sherry's voice gave me over the mile of wire.

Sherry said, "You boys. You never leave each other. You come back for the lost one. It's like a movie—"

"Well . . . we just . . ."

"No, no. A very good movie. The best I've ever seen."

Though it's not quite true, I tell everybody that was the moment I decided whom I was going to marry. I didn't exactly tell her, but I think she knew. I was so babbling and inarticulate I could hardly have meant anything else.

VIII

Tilden was known among us as "Mr. Christmas" because of his child-like attentiveness to every nuance of
the holidays, continuing long after he officially ceased to be
a child. He was the first to have those strings of tree lights
that looked like flames, or the tips of kindergarten pencils.
If one of the bulbs burned out, the whole string went dark,
so most of our Christmas trees would have negative spaces
where we had been too idle to seek for the faulty link—but
not Tilden's tree. It blazed and twinkled, for he would find
the dead bulb like a terrier finding a rat in the basement.
My dad's store supplied all this stuff, so I knew the details of
how much of Tilden's yard work money he spent on magical
Christmases. Those lights burned hot. Most of us dealt with
that by turning them off every so often, but Tilden found
reflectors made of aluminum, that made each bulb look like
the Bethlehem star, beamy and many-colored. You'd sweat
in the room with the tree, but you wouldn't worry the whole
thing would go up in smoke. The town had not been elec-
trified for that long, and Tilden's ease with the electric part
of Christmas made him a welcome guest up and down the
streets, helping to find shorts and dead bulbs, explaining
how things worked, helping to set up the tree so it wouldn't
burst into flames the first time the switch was flipped. Under his own tree he set little villages made of chips from
the wood pile, a metropolis of pioneers in tiny log cabins,

through which lights shone as if each had an enchanted fireplace of a different color. Toy animals were placed about to indicate farms and pets and, I suppose, the kind of outdoor zoo that would have obtained in Jesus's day. The lead army men he had gotten from his uncle stood about guarding things in their funny WWI hats. There was a pond made of a mirror laid amid cotton batting (which was snow) and on that mirror floated plastic swans. It was a little queer—of course we told him so—but it was also pretty wonderful. I hope we told him that, too. There were no big department stores in our town, and Dad's Santa in the hardware store window and the crèches in front of a couple of the churches were all the inspiration he had. It was a miracle, if you thought about it.

Tilden's Electric Wonderland is part of what materializes when I summon up Christmas. But what lingers most deeply is the perception of a single perfect Christmas, made from fragments of recollections cast over a period of ten or more years. There was but one Christmas, unfolding in a particular way we fashioned and enforced for ourselves over the whole of our boyhoods. The family tree must be decorated in a certain way, and you remembered from year to year what that way was. This bulb went here; that bulb went there. Variation was forgetfulness. Forgetfulness was the opening act of a sadness that grew through the years and would not be cured. We knew these things without being told. It was Yule, whose enchantments struck deeper even than the Nativity Story. You went to church. You sang the carols. You knew they were intimations of something vast and silent, something that needed to dwell in the mountains and the singing gorge of the Wyona, and could never quite come to town.

Christmas Eve was for families, and church. So the day before, or the day before that, we had our own ceremony, which seemed to have been ordained. Nobody that I remember organized a moment of it. Maybe we copied it off Andy's circle, or Dad's, or maybe it was a discovery of us ourselves. We peregrinated, like Magi, from house to house, taking in the food and the peculiarities of the family Christmases, as we took in the peculiarities of one another throughout the year.

We started at Vince's. We presented this to one another as a courtesy, and never spoke aloud the actual reason, which was that Mrs. Silvano typically hit the sauce around 7, and if we wanted her company at any level of consciousness, we had to have been there and gone. Unlike the other mothers, Mrs. Silvano did not bake, but she organized the store-bought cookies in artful ways, in concentric circles on the round plates (alternating dark and pale if that's what came out of the box) and in interesting ranks and files on the square ones, replacing one of the proper shade when one got devoured. Sometimes there would be bologna cut with cookie cutters in the shapes of stars and snowmen. These you could fold over onto a cracker or just put into your mouth whole. This was her understanding of proper hostessing, and we took it that way, admiring her skills and attentiveness from behind the rims of our glasses of orange punch. She had been Homecoming Queen in her time. We understood. Vince was allowed to call his mother a lush in moments of frustration, but we, never.

Coach was not present for these events. Sometimes he was upstairs—walking around on the wooden floors gave him away—but often his car would be gone and Mrs. Silvano would say he went to get something she needed, but whatever she needed must have been in Knoxville, for he didn't come back. Coach didn't spell "Christmas" to us, so it was all right. Getting together with the guys must have seemed pretty homo to him.

Tilden was next, and he'd be beside himself with excitement. We wouldn't be through the door yet, and he'd be showing us his newest gadget or setup, how he made his electric train go around and around the multicolored cabins, over the looking-glass lake, among the lead giraffes and doughboys and whatnot. He would have baked the cookies. He would have made the really amazingly good date bread that you could spread with oleo and jam from his mother's plum trees. His mom would be there to hand him things he needed, but it was his show. Tilden was a happy kid—a life without drama, so far as I could see—and I think his happiness spread from the Christmases he lit up as though he himself were the Christ Child. There he was, his red crew cut lit by the blazing tree lights, chomping on his own cookies, smiling, smiling. That boy was a mystery with all the doors open. I knew him better than anyone else in the world, and yet I didn't know him. He was clever that way.

My house was last because Mom was the best cook, and we had bunk beds in case things evolved into a sleepover. We gave our buddies our gifts when we got to my house, little things we'd made or bought at my dad's store, Dad conspiring in it by making me go do something else if one of my friends walked in, so it would all be a surprise. One year Vince gave me a flashlight. One year Tilden gave me one of his lead animals, a bison really too hefty for the scene under the tree, that holds down papers on my desk to this day. One year my mom took an art class down in Asheville (*that's* a whole other story) and I got her to teach me what she learned enough that when I took photos at the Falls, I could come back and color the prints with watercolors so they looked like faded and pastel versions of the real thing.

If it was snowing when we got to my house, it would be perfect. Nothing could go radically wrong for the whole year after if it was snowing when we got to my house. I think it always was.

Glen fit right in regarding the Christmas revels. We were a little older, and so the sacred things were no longer so sacred they couldn't be adapted a little. You had to pass Glen's house to get from Vince's to Tilden's, and we waved as we passed to Glen's mother and big sister standing on the stoop waving back at us. His father would be inside reading the paper beside a huge floor lamp, the Christmas tree across the room from him. This was right. This was the way it should be. The father should be sitting with the paper. The mother should be watching her boy and his friends pass through the snow onward into darkness. We didn't go in. The ritual was too set for that. Glen understood. He could fit in in his way, but not in all ways.

The temptation when the time came was to invite our girlfriends. We thought about it, but in the end we didn't. We said to one another, "Why would they be interested?" It was all pretty boyish. Sherry was the only of the girlfriends of the time who lasted, and she never batted an eyelid over her exclusion. If she wanted to come she never said so. In married life one learns that women long for their men to have buddies, hobbies, diversions, to go on camping trips and get the hell out of the house now and then. But then we admired them for being able to do without our company even for a couple hours.

If the three of us owned Christmas, Glen still found a way in. New Year's was open. That could be his, if he wanted it.

One New Year's remains frozen in memory. Glen had come to our houses before Christmas, eating the cookies, talking with the dads and moms who then made their courteous exits. He was the kind of teenager parents like, and would tell you so afterwards, his politeness and good vocabulary and all that. He'd bought us all Bowie knives as presents. This was at once very cool and very odd. Four Bowie knives with shellacked buckhorn handles, exactly alike. I pictured us striding through town with them stuck in our belts. It was not right to ask, "What the hell put this into your head?" but maybe it was his move to be as woodsy as the rest of us presumed ourselves to be. Plus, they were no odder, the Bowie knives weren't, than other things we'd opened under the twinkling tree through the years. Maybe it was that there were so many, a little arsenal in case some enemy should arise to take the place of the Japs and Krauts.

"I have another gift," Glen said.

Tilden looked around to see if it was under the tree.

I said, "What? You and Vince finally announcing your engagement?"

Vince didn't want to laugh, but finally did. But it was as if Glen hadn't heard. He continued, "It's for New Year's Eve. A little surprise. You gotta promise me New Year's Eve. All right?"

Vince said, "I'll call Lauren Bacall and tell her she's on her own this year."

So we promised Glen New Year's Eve. He handed the three of us envelopes. We opened them. They turned out to be three parts of a map to the Falls of the Wyona.

"We're going to the Falls?"

"Yeah. The surprise will be there."

"It'll be *freezing*," Tilden observed.

Glen said, "Wear a coat."

Glen had drawn the maps himself, and covered the corners with "*Hic sunt dracones*" and compass roses and things you find on ancient maps. I had the first part. He wanted us to start at the edge of the school grounds, where the long overland path to the gorge actually does start.

"Can't we drive?"

"We'll drive back. I'll have a car in the parking lot."

So on New Year's Eve the three of us lined up at the edge of the high school parking lot. That in itself was a dip into nostalgia. It had been a long time since we'd actually hiked to the Falls, and longer still since we hadn't used the various shortcuts and by-ways learned through the years. We were entering by the gate. We were going the full way. This turned out to be good, for the sights we saw that night were, altered by darkness and winter, the sights we saw the first time we had gone together to the Falls, hesitant, chattering like the children we were, unsure of the way. The swifts gathered in a cave in South America now, and the bats clung to the ceiling asleep. The salamanders dozed under the ice. We were alone, the first souls in a bewintered world, or the last.

Then into the wilderness.

It had snowed a couple of the days since Christmas. The snow turned pink because of the angle of the sun. It had melted in town, but here the snow was sheltered by the trees, which, though bare, shed a coolness around them winter as well as summer. Out of the crusty whiteness poked the skeletons of ironweed and Joe-pye, and deeper in, the ruined towers of the wood lilies, with their seed pods perching on them like winter birds. The actual birds left tiny thready tracks atop the crust, while the foxes and the deer fell through and dug furrows toward their night retreats. It was not that cold, despite Tilden's fears; soon I was sweating and had to open my jacket.

Vince said, "Wait." He plowed through the snow and plucked something off an old apple tree that was the last remnant of a farm that must have stood there generations ago. It was an envelope. On it was written, "Arden."

Vince handed the envelope to me. I opened it. Inside was a photo of me as a tiny, tiny boy in a fat snowsuit, so round and warm I could scarcely move. The hand reaching down to steady me ran off the edge of the paper, but I knew it was my mom. I was smiling. I was so, so happy. Maybe I had never been quite that happy since. I felt myself grinning in the gathering twilight.

Tilden said, "Cool. Move on?" I nodded. We moved on.

Tilden had the second section of the map, and though we knew the way, we opened it in case there was a message or a surprise. A big circle in orange crayon surrounded a black . . . thing that would have been a mystery to anybody else, but which we recognized instantly as the shelf stone. The shelf stone is a black monolith about twenty feet high, sticking right out of the roots of hemlocks, upon which, chest high when we first entered the woods, but waist high now, is a flat outcrop like a shelf. The resemblance to a pagan altar in a jungle movie was too great to ignore, so we always left something on the shelf—an apple or a candy—for the forest gods, and it was always gone when we passed by again. We made for the shelf stone—it was a little off the path. That part of the woods lay in shadow now, so Vince snapped on his flashlight. Something sat on the shelf. I walked over and turned a piece of paper to the light. The paper said "Tilden." The paper was held down by something, and when Vince turned the light on it we saw a line of carved animals, a horse and an antelope and a kangaroo, all beautifully wrought out of some heavy blond wood none of us could guess at. Tilden stared at them for a moment while Vince held them in the light. Then he put them in his pocket and we moved on.

At the point where Tilden's map failed, I took over the light and Vince looked at his third of the map. "It says we have to turn out the light when we hear the sound of the Falls."

I didn't like that much. I think we all heard the Falls before we acknowledged it, because it was almost full dark, and we had no light but that. But eventually Vince shrugged, and sighed, and turned out the light. I heard him say under his breath, "That boy—"

As our eyes adjusted we saw a couple of things. One was that the snow and the clear stars provided enough ambient light to keep us from running into things. The path that Glen had carved with his boots was a deeper blue in the blue-white of the snow field. We could follow it easy. Additionally, there appeared to be a source of light up ahead, different from the stars, less piercing, warmer, golden. When we got a few yards further on we saw that Glen had put candles in paper bags settled into the snow, and those were lighting the way. I touched one of the bags. It wasn't even hot. The snow must have balanced the heat of the flame. How had Glen known that and we not? Maybe a hundred of these torches set at intervals led us to a grove that we knew quite well—the excellent picnic grove—but that was changed somehow. We entered the grove. At the far end of it a living white pine had been festooned with candles, and the candles were burning. There was barely breeze enough to make them flicker, and Glen had chosen a place—as we often had—sheltered from the weather on all four sides. Glen stood beside the tree. He was difficult to see—all you could see were the little flames and the bit of pine branch nearest to them. He must have known this, so he moved into as much of the light as he could, and said, "Welcome."

The shellacked handle of a Bowie knife glittered in his belt.

My recollection is that one word. "Welcome" was the only one uttered. Glen had provided four logs, and we sat down on them and looked at the tree. Mom and Dad had candles on our tree when I was little. It sent me there. It sent me home. Yes. This was it. This was perfect. It was the best ever. It was the one thing that had yet happened in my life to which I would apply the word "holy."

We heard a low dragging sound. It was Vince moving his log so it was directly opposite Glen's. He sat back down. They were staring into each other's eyes. Glen put his hand out and Vince took it. They sat so the candlelight washed over them, as though that were the one thing it was meant to do. Eye to eye, hand in hand. I wondered why there had been no gift for Vince, but I understood now: this was it. The whole artifact was it. The walled garden, the tree of flames, the roof of stars—they were Glen's gift to Vince, lover to beloved. I was dropping tears onto the snow.

Vince said, "Wherever you go, I will find you."

Glen said, "Me too."

After that came such quiet you could hear the candle flames. Then we heard another sound, chuckling, funny-sounding, from low down in the darkness. I speculated that it was a gnome or something talking to itself—the atmosphere was conducive to such thought—but it came close and when it broke into the circle of light one perceived it was a skunk. Now, we were all woodsmen, so we knew a skunk is the calmest of creatures, totally hospitable unless you manage to frighten it. I was going to warn, "Don't get up, don't run," but nobody seemed inclined to do so. Our little friend waddled from log to log, nosing at our clothes to see what manner of creatures we might be in the dead of a winter night with the little fires around us. When he was satisfied, he waddled off, chuckling and singing to himself, until his black and white faded into the ink blue of the undergrowth. The forest had blessed us. The spirits had taken form and communed with us for a precious moment.

Glen got up after a few moments and said, "Onward."

The roar of the Falls felt tremendous after the quiet of the grove. Glen led us to the brink, and then down a bit of path to a place we knew that overlooked almost the whole drop of the Falls, from the crest to the secret bottom, a little less secret now for its ice and glinting snows. The path should have been slick, and I kept bracing myself, but it became clear that Glen had thought of that too, breaking the ice—with his boot heel, I guess—and scattering it before we arrived. We'd stood there for maybe ten minutes when the light changed. The Wyona flows from the east, so at its far end there was a conflagration of pink and orange, piercing through the hundred mile tangle of trees. While we watched, the moon hove above the horizon, blood red, and then flamingo, then orange, then rising shell-pink until it reigned in snow whiteness in the middle of the sky. It was a half moon only, but it drowned the darkness in a flood of light. It hit the top of the Falls and turned it into a fountain of pearl. Vince and Glen embraced. Tilden and I embraced, and then we made the rounds until everybody had been embraced, singly and communally.

Tilden said the fourth thing that had been said, "This is the best night ever."

We assumed it was past midnight and another year. It was getting cold, and my toes were a little numb. We turned back. We gathered the candles from the tree, and dumped snow in the candle-bags, meaning to come for them in the morning. We took a different way, for Glen had brought his car so we wouldn't have to walk back, though maybe, considering it all, we should have. The moon would then have come to the middle of the sky, and turned the Falls from top to bottom into a pillar of diamond. We knew. We didn't have to see. The same moon lit up the parking lot with blue clarity. There was Glen's car all right, but another one beside it, one with its motor running. A cloud of steam came from the exhaust. When we entered the open space the doors of the car opened.

Vince said, "Fuck."

There in the dome light stood Coach. Out of the back seats came a couple of the Varsity guys, looking sleepy and confused, but ready to do whatever Coach demanded. Innocent Tilden said, "Happy New Year, Coach—" and began walking toward him. Coach passed him on the pavement without a sign. He was making for Vince. I had absolutely no idea of what to do. I prayed to Jesus he had come there to wish his son Happy New Year. Unmistakable in the moonlight, Coach shot out his arm and said, "What the hell is this?" I couldn't see what he meant, what he was holding in his hand. Neither could Vince, or at least Vince made no reply. Frustrated by the night, Coach wadded up the thing in his hand and threw it so it hit Vince in the face. It was paper. It fell to the frost at their feet.

"Boy, I asked you a question. What the fucking hell—"

"I'm not going with you, Dad. I'm going with Glen."

"Like fuck," Coach said. He motioned behind him without turning around. The bruisers from the back seat ran forward. Vince turned to run, but Coach was on him like the panther he was, dropping him to the pavement. Coach was steel and sinew, and I could hear Vince's head crack on the ground. He stopped fighting. The other two came up and held me and Tilden off. I had no idea what was going on, so I couldn't get the fight up in me. Besides, the capability of hitting one of our friend's dads was not in us. Glen moved forward out of the shadows, but one of the linebackers crumpled him with one punch. Then they were gone.

I picked the wad of paper Coach had thrown off the frost and put it in my pocket. Glen drove us home. Tilden kept chattering, "What? What? What?" but Glen was silent. When I was home and emptying my pockets, I found the paper. It had dried in my pocket on the ride home, though in places it had smeared a little. I opened it and read. It was a letter from Glen to Vince:

Dear Vince,

   You must have figured out it's me putting these notes in your locker. Or, if you have more than one admirer, just don't tell me. I will try to be content with your kisses. I will try to be content hearing you tap my window in the dead of night, opening, feeling you sink into my arms. You smell of the tree, you know, the tree you have to climb to get in my window. I like that. You know what I like better? On the gorge rim by starlight, with the Falls roaring around us and the swifts flying out at first light, you and I body to body, heart to heart. I still can't believe that you love me. I'm trying to find the lamp I rubbed to make this wish. I wonder sometimes what would happen if your dad found out, but he's so stupid we could do it in front of him and he wouldn't know. Word is he does it with his players, so maybe it's all right. I want you to know something. If we ever get separated . . . if we ever get parted, you'll know where to find me. If you want me, come. Come find me. I will wait until you come, for I know you will come. If you want us to be a secret, we can start there, we can start again in the most secret place in all the world. I will not come back unless you come for me. I know you will come. I feel you will come. Nothing else matters.

Your Glen

We had four days before school started up after Christmas vacation. We needed every one of them to decide what to do. In the end we did nothing. Vince appeared at school with a shiner and a small bandage and shaved space on the back of his head. We sat together at the café table as if nothing had happened, talking about everything but that. We didn't see Glen for weeks. Tilden had access to the typed-up school roll (being an office helper during first period), and reported that Glen Copland was out of town with his parents, an excused absence. When he came back we knew only because he disappeared from the absence roll. He didn't come to us. He didn't seek us out. He merely reappeared. I smiled to him in the hall as if he were a new kid again, and had never met. He smiled back.

I packed the Bowie knife away in the top of my closet. It looked like there would never now be an occasion to use it. I still had the wrapping paper and the bag it came in. I really hadn't looked at everything in the bag when I opened the present—you know how kids are. Folded in there was a sheet of handwritten stationery. I think it was something

Glen had dropped in to give me a little flavor of himself—he being a little hard to get at in the normal ways. In the same handwriting of the fatal note Coach threw in the parking lot was the following:

—found slender cliffbrake in a wet seam right where the river goes over. Wyona builds a roof of spray to protect it. Cool. Cool as a glacier. Three, four tiny little stalks. In a thousand miles there'll be no other, I think. The light shows through them green on the white stone behind. Mr. Berg says it only grows in the north and that I must have misidentified something else. I ask it what it is. It tells me. Slender Cliffbrake.

Bracken.

Hart's tongue.

Spleenwort.

Wall rue.

Slender cliffbrake.

Arden likes the flowers. They grow where it's dry. I find him flowers and he smiles.

Rose mallow.

Corn cockle.

Evening primrose.

I wrote "club moss" down but had to scratch it, because it's not a flower.

Climb down to the bottom. The ferns would hate it if they had ears, all that noise. *Bruuuuuuuuuuu*—forever and forever, like a Hindu praying. *Bruuuuuuuuuuu*. I climb down to the bottom. I keep saying that sentence to myself, "I climb down to the bottom." It must mean something more. I keep repeating it because I don't get it. I'm not supposed to be here by myself. Horsetail in the quiet backwaters of the pool. I stay long enough to watch the swifts come home. I'll be afraid in the dark climbing back up, but it's worth it. Watch carefully. I watch carefully where they home, the zillion birds. Listen, there's a hole in the water. Part of the cliff sticks out, and there's a hole in the Falls under it, twice as tall as me, and no wider. Thousands and thousands all pass through. I climbed to the bottom and now I must go in. If you go careful around the rim it's OK. Slippery, but OK. Liverworts I'll have to come back for. Hold onto the wall with two hands. It's not big, though, not very big. The pool will let you go around. Then I stood there. I stood at the door, smelling, listening. I whispered pretty quietly into the door in the water, "I've climbed to the bottom now." I wish I hadn't. There is someone there. There is someone in the cave under the falls.

Cut myself climbing. Kept looking back. Everyone says you shouldn't go there by yourself. Now I know why.

I dialed six of the numbers to Glen's phone. I set the receiver down before I dialed the seventh.

IX

The grounds crew left the hoses out on the field. They'd been watering the grass, and something else came up, or they got distracted when the cheerleaders came out to hone their routines. The marching band was out there practicing their hearts out, stepping over the hoses, tripping on the hoses, tooting their tubas. Coach regarded the marching band with real hatred, which was funny because they existed for no other reason than to exalt him. Maybe he thought they took too much attention away at halftime. We watched him watching them with the familiar rictus of contempt on his face. Then something happened. The rictus changed into a sly grin, which on Coach was really rather terrifying. He motioned his boy Vinny and Gordy Merritt over and whispered something into their ears. We saw them jog to the sidelines. We watched. What were they doing? In a minute we understood. On signal, they both turned the water on at the same instant, and it came spraying out of the nozzles, right underneath the band. The band broke ranks and fled for their lives, trying to hold their precious instruments away from the water. It was choice. It was really, really choice.

Rickenbacker High made the playoffs again that year. Big surprise. Coach nearly always aced the local champ, but the conference had lately extended down into Buncombe

County, where we faced the big County and the Asheville City schools, and out past Nantahala, where massive boys came out of the narrow hollers with murder on their fearsome brains. Something about growing up in the wilderness put the wild animal into a kid. They were saved and church-going, and would rip your head off at the toot of a whistle. We were up to it. With Coach at our head, we were inspired to win and terrified not to.

Sherry and I attended the inter-varsity dance parties the Athletes for Christ set up so the kids from the various schools could meet one another. A mixer, they called it at college. The dances were sock hops, where you took off your shoes and danced to Nelson Riddle and the Dorseys on the gym floor. Most of the local churches didn't like dancing, so the fact that there were records and a record player present set the right tone of gentle rebelliousness. You had to dance a certain distance from the Victrolas, or the records would jump. The AFC get-togethers were thoroughly jockey. Though tacitly invited, regular kids never went, only the athletes and their buddies and their girlfriends. The Jesus sock hops were unexpectedly sensually charged. They were flirt-fests, and though they were not advertized that way, everyone knew. The girls dashed home to change after school and came rushing back dressed in intriguing compromises between cheerleader and cocktail lounge chanteuse. The boys stopped at their lockers to douse themselves in cologne. Sherry, who was a Unitarian, was a little apprehensive before the constant and vivid display of born-again faith, but she went through it for the team's sake. The honor of praying over the cold sandwiches and the coke went to the host team, and part of the honor was deriving a prayer of exceeding length and eloquence. If the coke was not flat when the praying was over, someone had not done his job.

You could say anything you wanted if you added "In Jesus' name" or "to God be the Glory." You could express in prayer the wish to grind the opposing team into the dirt if it could be to God's glory, or vaunt your own splendor on the field if all you did was done in Jesus' name. You'd say "praise God" where in ordinary conversation you'd say "uh" or "fuck," and the ease of transition between the worldly mode and the transcendent seemed to be the mark of the advanced Christian.

After an initial period of unfamiliarity, Sherry was delighted with it all. A change of pressure from her hand onto mine would signal when something especially notable was going on. Jonathan Mick, the big fullback from Mountain Heritage, was praising his girlfriend to her face. She was a looker, all right, her pink sweater straining at the seams and her hair dyed a flaming orange. Her name almost had to be Missy. Anyway, Mick, instead of pointing out how hot she was (as if he needed to), said, "I honor the good work that God is doing in my girlfriend Missy," and everyone nodded as if they thought that's what he really meant. How we kept straight faces I don't know. I didn't worry so much about how to take all the crap with Sherry there. She thought it was all funny, without judgment or cynicism, and her view cleansed mine. The room brimmed with girls who were officially the most attractive in their schools, cheerleaders and homecoming queens. Sherry was the only one who wore no angora and had no aspirations toward the cheerleading squad. She was the only one who could have named the capital of South Carolina. I wouldn't have traded her for anyone. She seemed more substantial, older than the rest of them, and the only one who had not moth-balled her sense of humor for the sacred event.

Vince came late, after practice was over. He did not dog practice anymore, as we varsity heroes sometimes did, and stayed late to drill the laggards. Being the apple of his father's eye rather than a big disappointment was something he began to savor. He had not had time to clean up and douse himself with cologne, and one caught a glimpse of Sheila Gorman waylaying him in the hall to rub grime off his face and smooth his hair with her hand. He had to bend down to give her access, and the moment was quite beautiful, like a scene from a sentimental vignette or an old movie. Sherry was watching too. She laid her head on my shoulder and we watched a man we jointly loved perform an act of unconscious grace. That's what the Christians should have been talking about.

Vince had changed since the New Year's night nobody talked about. Sherry, without knowing anything of the details, said it was as though he had come in out of the night. His voice was louder. His hair was brilliantined. His shoes were shined. He wore his dad's championship ring on a finger beside his own. He'd always dated, but now he was dating through the crème de la crème, using up the A-list girls one at a time as though his curiosity and sexual restlessness had become insatiable. He dipped into B and C list, and his attentions raised these girls up. He was the captain of the football team. He was the quarterback. He possessed his father's swoon-inducing handsomeness. He became the stereotypical high school heartthrob that was within a decade of being immortalized on TV. Even I forgot the feel of the New Year's night on the mountain, assuming all that had been a phase that my friend was out of now, all whisked away by the hand of the Ordinary.

It was better this way, for Glen to be history and everyone else to be the way they were supposed to be. I'd enlarged my life to include Glen, but it had been an effort, and I didn't want to know about that anymore. Glen came to my house like we were old friends, and when I was with him, I liked him. Mom and Dad liked him. If Mom were cooking he would dice the onions. He did everything wrong and still you liked him, a little, though you were never disappointed when he went away. You can't have a friend who's an issue every single minute. It had been a phase. Nice, but over. Glen seemed to sense this and faded into the periphery.

Vince and his Sheila entered just as the prayer began. The Chosen build up quite an appetite, and nine delivery boxes balanced precariously on the lab table. They couldn't be opened until they were prayed over. After a moment of hesitant expectation, Steve Jenkleman strode out of the crowd, his countenance beaming with the pride of being that day's thanks-giver. Jenkleman and I had gone through the grades together, but our paths diverged as he grew into a behemoth evidently intended by God to be a linebacker. Jenkleman's forearms were famous. He wore short sleeves because his muscles would not accommodate too much cloth around them. He was stupid, too, but not quite as stupid as the expression of lobotomized beatitude he wore for the moment made him seem. I could tell through her grip on my arm that Sherry was mocking him with a goofy angel face of her own. I dared not look at her.

Jenkleman bowed his head, closed his eyes. A voice from somewhere in the crowd reminded us, "All heads bowed. All eyes closed." I bowed my head but I didn't close my eyes.

We Episcopalians didn't take instructions for our prayers. Jenkleman took a deep breath and recited what I took to be the accepted litany of things to be prayed about by such people upon such an occasion. He took a second breath, and the tone changed a little:

"And Lord, in the Name of Jesus Christ Thy Son Our Lord and Savior, we pray for Coach Silvano, thy servant, that he might overcome all interferers, all opposition, that the morons and bureaucrats who are always trying to slow him down be confused in their . . . in their efforts. Allow him to shine forth as the example to us of manhood, sportsmanship . . . and uhm . . . and Christian witness, and may he be rewarded the victory for thy son's glorious sake. In thy most blessed name, we beseech you from our hearts. Amen."

There was a moment of silence, then a great bending back of cardboard lids.

Sheila was history in about a week. Vince had to go out of town to find the next girl, a senior from Jonesboro, who had been in a beauty pageant and sometimes wore her tiara.

I overheard Vince and Tilden talking in the locker room. The end of Tilden's sentence as I walked in was, "—your dad must be so damn proud."

"Maybe he is. It's hard to tell."

"Look, when you decide, tell me. I want to go where you go. I want to play for the team you play for."

Vince said, "You got it, man."

Tilden wasn't good enough that the same school that gave Vince a scholarship would give him one. I thought of this with a measure of cruel satisfaction, from which I recoiled almost immediately. I stood there in the locker room thinking about why I'd sneered at my friend's hopes. It was because I'd decided against continuing football, maybe even against college. I would be happy running the hardware store. I knew that. But I was jealous that Tilden might be with Vince and I not. Vince had his father's glamour that way, that even when you disapproved of him, you wanted to be with him.

When Glen's dad came to our house, and Mom had let him in and called me down from my room, I didn't know who he was. I'd only seen him through the window, reading, or heard his voice from the interior of his house, bidding his son farewell when he came out to the wilderness with us. But I was well trained, and extended my hand and said, "Happy to see you, sir." Then I waited.

There was a long pause. Finally he realized the problem. "Oh. I'm his dad. I'm Gene Copland. I'm Glen's father."

Fuck, I thought deep inside my brain.

We sat in the living room, and Gene Copland asked me how my school year was going and whether I was thinking about college and whatnot. His manner was so like my own father's that I thought there must have been some manual for growing up in their generation, the likes of which was conspicuously missing from mine. He'd served in the Pacific, and had a big red scar from elbow to shoulder where shrapnel got him. "I was too old," he said, "too old and slow to get out of the way. They should have seen that at the recruitment center." He smiled. It was a joke. I smiled back at him. Like all boys my age, I was interested in the war, and led him to talk about the Zeros, as much as you can remember when you're diving into trenches to get away from them.

The war stories were over. Mr. Copland sat for a moment with his hands in his lap.

Finally he said, "Glen says you're his only friend."

"No, no sir, there are at least four of us and I assure you—"

"The only friend who understands. He says you still smile at him in the hall."

Only then did I realize what an insufficient gesture that was.

"He—" Mr. Copland shrugged. I couldn't help him, because I honestly had no idea what he was going to say.

"When I was about seventeen," he said, taking a different tack, "I met his mother. Mrs. Copland. Ruth. I think you met her."

"Yes sir."

"Meeting her may not prepare you for what I'm about to say. People look at one person and see different things. She's . . . she's not a movie star by any means. I know that. But when I met her . . . I hope you understand what I'm saying. I hope you have somebody like that, or will before too long. Glen says you have a girl, right?"

"Yes. Sherry."

"Good. Excellent. Keep her, if you can. The love of one's youth—anyway when I met Ruthie it was like being thrown down onto the ground. The bomb blast that did this to my arm was nothing in comparison. I loved her . . . so much. She was a bomb that exploded every morning when I woke and thought of her. She didn't notice me at first. We come from St. Louis, and society is . . . uhm . . . stratified there, and I wasn't the sort of person she would look at. If she did, there would be plenty of people to set her straight and find her somebody . . . more suitable. But I . . . I wouldn't take no for an answer. Actually I took no for an answer about a hundred times . . . but I kept coming on back . . . and back. I knew Ruthie was the one person I was going to love in my life, the one and only, and that I would love her forever, and it just wasn't fair for her to go through life without that. I don't know how I won, but I did, and Ruthie and I . . . will go through all this to the end."

He raised his hands up, palms flat at "all this," to indicate the universe and eternity.

"So when Glen said to me that he . . . that he had found somebody, and that it looked impossible, I told him all this. I told him he must never give up. He must try everything. He had to let 'no' or 'get lost' run off him like rain from a duck's back. Arden, he never told me it was . . . he never told me it was another man. There was nothing in . . . nothing in the way he was around us to indicate that. This Vince would come to our house . . . by day he'd use the door just like everybody else. Nice boy. Always with the wisecracks. But at night he would come . . . and not use the door. Glen's window would open and close . . . there would be whispering. If they had been younger, I would have thought nothing. But . . . I knew. After a time. I said nothing, but I knew."

I was trying to have no reaction at all. He noted this and went on. "I wasn't used to it. I didn't know what to say. But I don't think I could have given him any other advice, though. Anything other than what I said. If this is what he wanted—so bad—" Mr. Copland shrugged. "He is very unhappy."

"I know."

"Can you help him?"

"You tell me how and I'll do it."

"This Vince . . . he's the same way?"

"Looks like. At least where Glen's concerned."

"So there is hope?"

"Not while Coach is alive."

Copland's shoulders sagged. He looked small and old sitting in my dad's chair. "Then be his friend, Arden. If you can, just be his friend."

I said I would. Mr. Copland shuffled out into the evening. I had lied. I didn't know how to be Glen's friend anymore. I was Vince's friend first, and if Vince was backing away, so was I.

While Glen went ghosting through the halls, clinging to the walls like a rat, the rest of us rode high. She ran every third committee and club, and I joined them, even, ludicrously, the French club, to be near her. Coach was so happy to have his boy back that he often forgot to be cruel, and we looked surreptitiously at each other at the end of practices where he hadn't prescribed five laps of wind sprints before we could go home. Vince dated Carmen, who was in the fashion vanguard by having her peroxide hair piled up onto her head like a triton shell, and teased and sprayed so that even a full body tackle wouldn't dislodge it. She must have picked that up from the summer she spent with an aunt in Charlotte. I was pleased with myself because I sowed love all around me, heaps of it on Sherry and Vince and Tilden and Andy and Mom and Dad, but even great handfuls on the kids I passed in the halls or rammed bone against bone in scrimmage. Someone who has a relationship with God should tell Him how much better people are when they are happy. I know the saints are meant to be good and kind even when they're sick and miserable, but that's too much to ask of most of us. My goodness extended to visiting the Coplands every now and then. I'd sit in the kitchen and talk with his mom and dad. They were always sorry that Glen, somehow, wasn't home—as if he had a life and could conceivably be somewhere else. I figured he was there and just couldn't face me. That got old after a while, and I stopped the visits, though I always waved when I passed by on the way to Tilden's, so they'd know I was thinking of them.

Tilden got to Advanced Physics and something clicked with him. I was sitting beside him when he "got" it. I heard a swift intake of breath, like someone preparing to be sick, and turned and saw Tilden beaming rays of comprehension the likes of which nobody had seen before. He raised his hand. He answered the question Mr. Schmitz had already asked fruitlessly seven times. The answer was right. Tilden asked a follow-up, the answer to which had to be looked up, because teacher didn't know. Mr. Schmitz had to sit down and calm himself. After class, Schmitz marched Tilden down to the counselors' office and picked him up a college application and made him fill it out. In thirty years of teaching, Helmut Schmitz had never had a protégé until that very hour. He loved Tilden with a love pure and radiant. Tilden went up and down the halls saying to everyone who'd listen, "I'm going to be a physicist."

Tilden was easy to love. It was like sitting beside a campfire. He provided occasion to contemplate blessing and privilege. Tilden was blessed. Good, one thought, because he was one's friend. But why Tilden and not somebody else? Why not Timmy who fell down the Falls? Why not Clarence who fell down the Falls? Why not those Jewish kids listening in cellars for the tread of Nazi boots? Would I take the blessing away from Tilden until all could be explained to my satisfaction? Hell no. At that point I let the cosmos hoard its mysteries. Tilden could go ahead and be happy if that's what God wanted.

On the other hand, big brother Andy seemed to be in a holding pattern, dating a few local girls, working down at Dad's store, something which he never liked but never complained about. He was pale and quiet. You could cuddle him and be near him, but part of the pleasure was gone because he didn't seem to notice in particular. You think soldiers will come home from victory with their chests puffed out crowing like cocks of the walk, but that didn't happen to Andy. I began to gather it didn't happen much at all except in the movies.

The one thing that brought a spark to him was when Chief Dadlez pulled, as the saying was then, a boner, when he did something stupid or was quoted in some stupid comment in the regional paper. That got Andy fired up in a way that was not easy to understand. Andy wasn't a mocker (I am; it's one of the many ways I must have been a disappointment to my parents) nor were his comments about Dadlez mockery, but rather a sort of indignation, as though something important and solemn were being misrepresented. He hadn't got himself blown up in an Italian wheat field so fools could strut around making stupid comments. He'd rehearse his objections in front of Mom at the breakfast table. She'd nod and agree, and this might have given Andy the conviction that his objections made universal sense. One day, at his patience's end and bolstered by Mom's tacit agreement, he roared down to the two-room police station and laid his grievances before Chief Dadlez. I would like to have been a fly on the wall for that one. I told him he was going to get himself arrested, but I was wrong. Andy came back with a silver badge and a pamphlet that would help him study for the police officer's exam. Dadlez had shut him up by hiring him.

Something had kept Andy from saying, "I want to be a cop," or us from saying it for him, which was odd, because we all must have seen he would make a good one, what with his quiet patience, his strength, his kindness. I guess we thought he'd go away and make something of himself in a big city somewhere. No. He wanted to stay home. He wanted to stay home and protect those he loved. He was the biggest homebody in the world, and our grand designs for him had not let him admit it. Within six months he was a full-fledged cop, Dadlez's heir apparent, and married to Neetha, Tilden's big sister, which made Tilden and me brothers-in-law, which was very, very cool. They had been sweethearts in high school, but when the war came many threads were broken. Some could be rewoven. Andy the cat had fallen a long time, but at last had landed on his feet.

You look for the ratchet to make it all stay, to keep it all from falling back.

September. The high hills southward were getting their first color. Coach had some paperwork for me to look at, so I was late getting to the shower after practice. I came into the locker room toweling off. When I pulled the towel off my head I saw Vince sitting on the bench in front of his locker, looking at the floor.

"V," I said.

"Ardo."

"Thought you were long gone."

"Nope."

"You waiting for your dad?"

"Not really. Just—"

"Waiting?"

"Yeah."

"He was easy on us today."

Vince harrumphed.

I toweled a little at the back my neck. "So, have you heard yet?"

"What do you mean?"

"Tennessee. Chapel Hill—"

The team stars had been waiting for offers from colleges. One of the traditions of the squad was not to talk about offers, because it seemed braggedy and those who hadn't gotten any would feel bad. But you could ask, and if you asked the lucky boy could tell.

"Yeah, them. Western. Waiting for Duke, but I don't really want to go there."

"Still, you got a choice."

"UNC probably won't start me. Tennessee will. That might be the choice."

"Excited?"

"Trying to be, Ardo. You?"

"Got a couple of phone calls. I said no."

"You're pretty fed up with football, no?"

"Yeah. Nobody's fault, though."

"Yes it is. My dad's. I want to keep going just to see what it would be like to play for somebody who isn't insane."

I laughed. Only Vince would dare say that. Vince had his pants off but a white singlet still on, like he'd been knocked unconscious for a second while trying to undress.

"Better hurry. Coach is going to turn the hot water off."

"There'll be plenty. Ardo?"

"Yeah?"

"We alone?"

"I think so."

"I don't feel the way I should. I don't feel—"

"What? You don't feel what?"

"Happy. I should be happy. Everything's going exactly the way"—he paused so long I was starting to say something, but then he added—"it should."

"Carmen is choice," I said, mentioning his current squeeze.

"Carmen *is* choice. It's not that."

It wasn't football either. Vince's touch was golden. Nothing on the field went wrong for him. It wasn't academics; Coach had all the teachers trained so they just passed him along. I thought I knew what it was but I, by God, wasn't going to say it.

Vince tugged at the singlet so that was off too. "Is Andy going to marry Tilden's sister?"

"Looks like."

"I wish I had a sister. You could marry her."

"I would, too." For the moment, friendship was more important than reminding him of Sherry. I loved Vince. Seeing him there kind of crumpled up and vulnerable made me love him tenderly, like I should go and hold him for a minute. Of course I didn't.

Vince touched the tip of his dick, lovingly, as though preparing it for the shock of the shower. I said, "Think of all the girls that would pay cash money to be where I am, watching Vince Silvano with his pants off."

He smiled a huge smile. Then I ruined it. I went too far. I swear I wasn't thinking of anything but the next joke when I said, "Plenty of guys, too."

Vince's face collapsed before he burst into tears. Really sobbing. I stood there toweling my stupid ass while my best friend sobbed on the locker room bench. I went and turned a shower on real hard, so if somebody were still there besides us, they wouldn't hear.

X

For Homecoming that year the Boosters made a gigantic bonfire on the football field. They put up crepe paper and paper flowers like it was a prom, and hired a band, and the mayor was there, and a state representative, and more journalists than was good for a town like ours. Tables of cold cuts and loaves of bread were laid out under the half moon. Vats of pink punch sat unprotected from the surreptitious flasks of revelers. Dogs raced and barked between people's legs. Baby sisters and brothers toddled in the long grass. The team was got up in our red and gold varsity sweaters, each with a golden cardboard crown on our head to underline the truth that we were the kings of the world. The principal threw a football to Coach and Coach threw it to Vince and Vince threw it to some pretty girl in the crowd. She caught it, and that seemed to all a fine omen. Speeches broke out here, old time fight songs and alma maters. They sang the UT alma mater because everyone thought Vince was going there. It was wonderful. Carmen made sure to maneuver herself and her hair and Vince as close to the bonfire as they could, to make sure of being perpetually in the light. Andy parked his patrol car at the edge of the firelight. He'd say it was to give everyone a sense of security, but it was actually so he could drink in the excitement, the innocence, the great fire that was not a city burning.

Lightning flashed way off to the west. It would take a while to get to us, if it came at all.

The punch was spiked like mad. Each spiker thought he was the first. We had more than we actually wanted, lifting the tin cups higher and higher, to savor the image of ourselves drinking to a stupor barefaced before teachers and parents.

At some point, Glen walked out of the crowd. Sherry saw him and elbowed me. I was afraid at first, but the look on him was beneficent. The glow of hero-worship beamed from his face when he looked at Vince, but in that he was no different from anybody else in the milling crowd. What was different is that he walked up to Vince in the scarlet and golden firelight, pushed Carmen gently to one side, and kissed him on the lips.

For a moment it looked like it was going to be all right. The part of the crowd that could see Vince and Glen fell silent in the first seconds, but here and there tinkled forth a titter of laugher, and it could have been that everyone would laugh it off as some drunken overstatement of enthusiasm, even a kind of nerd satire. There was not a man in the school who didn't want to kiss Vince that night. I couldn't imagine what thoughts were coursing through their minds, either of them. I held my breath. I saw Vince come to a decision. He pulled back his bullet-pass right arm and slugged Glen in the face. Glen staggered and went down on one knee. Over all the sounds of bonfire and reveling and the tentative upsurge of laughter, Vince shouted, "YOU GET THE FUCK AWAY FROM ME, YOU QUEER!"

The team closed in around Vinny as though he had been in danger. One lifted Glen up to his knees; another gut-punched him so he fell backward into the dust again. This wasn't going to stop. Another picked him up. A heavy foot launched toward Glen's chest. A line began to form. The laughter stopped.

My mom had a cat named Randy who could vanish into thin air. He'd do something wrong, and you'd go to swat at him, and he'd disappear. You'd be looking where he was, and suddenly he was not. Turned to atoms. Glen did that. At some point when the team paused to take a breath, I saw him get up from the ground, but then he seemed to dematerialize, as though he had been made of mist. I should have followed him, but, honest to God, I didn't know it was going to be such a big deal. It's not like they'd never kissed before. It's not like I hadn't seen Vince drag Glen to the ground so he could cover him with himself and his kisses in the flickering woods. But when I realized that it was war and not love, I was not sure whose side I was on.

Sherry and I went from the bonfire to her parents' house. Her parents weren't home. It was like the beginning of a movie. We went up to her room. She kissed me hard. I think she was trying to figure out what Glen had done that lit Vince's rage so instantly. She was a girl, though. She would never understand men and what things must remain secret among us.

When I got home that gray morning, Mom still sat up, to report that I'd gotten, like, twenty phone calls from Glen's family wondering if I knew where he was. I said simply, "No," thinking they might never need to know the details. Glen would tell them when he was ready. Tilden called, and then some others, all with the same query.

It did not immediately occur to us to go looking. We pictured Glen licking his wounds somewhere, expecting to see him Monday morning as covert and hidden as ever.

Tilden hadn't seen the incident, but I told him and he said, "Whew." Both of us assumed Glen had not grown out of a phase that Vince had, and it all could be put down to a lack of communication. Tilden phoned Vince to see if he knew where Glen was. Vince said, "I hope he's dead, the little queer."

Monday came and Glen had not appeared. For fifteen minutes that was the talk in the halls. When 8 a.m. came according to the hall clocks, and the bells had not rung for homeroom, we began to get agitated. But some collective gravity started to draw us to the tiled lobby in front of the offices, where the cabinets full of trophies—most of them Coach's—gleamed in the light from the constantly opening and closing front doors. A crowd gathered. In the center of the lobby was a sturdy podium, and on top of the podium a box . . . like a radio, but different from a radio. Only a few of us who'd been to Knoxville or DC realized that what we were looking at was a television. The principal was standing behind the podium. He raised his hand and fiddled with something on the front of the box, and a light sprang up. The light grew, and then condensed, and shadows appeared in the flat circle of light. We arranged ourselves so that everyone could see, over or under or through someone's arms. The shadows thickened and sharpened until they were shapes. They were—it was hard to say. Sound came with the pictures, like it did in the movies, but the sound was too weak to hear back where I stood. There was a thing with one huge tooth . . . and a woman . . . two of them were puppets. Someone shouted backwards over the murmurs "It's Kukla,

Fran, and Ollie." It was Martian as far as I was concerned, but it was wonderful, too.

Television . . . television . . . I tried the new word in my mouth.

The principal let the picture run until it began to break up. Someone touched the box and the picture came back for a moment, but the signal was just too weak. The principal stepped in front of the podium and said, "I want you to remember this. It is the start of a brave new world." I kinda liked him for a moment; he seemed so excited, so sincere. Had one been close enough one might have seen a tear in his eye.

One did not think of it then, but Kukla, Fran, and Ollie flushed Glen Copland out of our heads. Tilden got the job of standing in the lobby for the rest of the day explaining how the television worked. Turned out he actually knew.

Nobody blamed Vince for being full of himself. He was the Man of the Century, as far as Eddie Rickenbacker High was concerned. There was no point in his even taking midterms, though he did, as a gesture of courtesy. I thought he overdid the kiss-indignation a tad, but his emotions, and his expression of them, could be extreme. The Silvanos were one of few Italian families in town, and we cut them slack when it came to emotions. I loved him. Lots of people would notice before I did when he hardened and soured.

Maybe I did see it. The number of people who could be called "queer" with that famous Silvano sneer expanded. Sherry didn't like to double date with him and Carmen any more.

I thought everybody was overdoing Victory Rally night. Glen probably just misjudged the moment. He might even have been joking.

Chief Dadlez marked Glen down as a runaway. I might have done the same thing, to have some finality to it, to prevent the daily trek of Mr. and Mrs. Copland down to the station asking, with their undertoned politeness that was somehow scarier than rage, whether he had found their boy. Sherry kept suggesting we check the Falls, but he wasn't the type, Glen wasn't. Some liverwort would have stopped his morbidity in its tracks. Glen's grandparents lived in St. Louis, and they were tried, but they had not seen him. They kept the porch lights on, but after a while there was little hope. As for me, I was anxious every day for a while, a week or so, as though there were something I could do to help find him and I wasn't doing it, some knowledge I had that could be helpful that I was failing to draw forth. Then one day that stopped. It's not that I stopped thinking about Glen, but rather that wherever he was had gone beyond my doing anything about it. Andy shrugged when he was asked his opinion about all this, as if he had no better idea. If he didn't, nobody did.

Vince laid low for a while, coming to school only for the vital classes he had to have for eligibility. On the same day I felt an odd, mystical release from Glen and his ghost, Vince showed up at school looking like he had just stepped from the pages of a fashion magazine. It was good to know we were on the same wavelength.

I talk about Vince as though he were separate from us. In some ways, maybe he was, but that's not how the masses of Rickenbacker High would have seen it. To be honest, we were a gang, a pack of broad-shouldered bruisers perpetually clumped together in places of public resort. We were kind of attractive, and everybody was proud of us, but you get a pack of young athletic males together and you risk energy overload, and when those young men admire each other chiefly for warrior attributes, you have a potential problem. We ourselves wouldn't have noted it, but we were a pride of hellcats to the unpopular kids. Some of us were bullies. We were all bullies in a way, for if some of us weren't active scourges, our chief reaction to the brutality of our brothers was to watch and laugh. Let me admit it never seemed other than the natural order of things, acknowledged by all sides. If Vinny got to call Allen Betts "Porky," Allen got to be called "Porky" by the school hero, who otherwise wouldn't have noticed him at all. Judy Herman, whom we called "Muffin" because her acne made her look like her face was studded with raisins, would otherwise pass through the halls unknown and unmarked. I'm not defending the custom, but defining it. What would have caused us to question this order of reality unless one of us crossed over to the other side? None of us ever did.

I say, on the day I lost spiritual touch with Glen, Vince returned to school full-time. From that day forward he seemed different. Glamorous. He stopped running with Tilden and me so much, and that gave us a little room to stand back and take perspective. Maybe he had always been glamorous, and we were so close to him we didn't notice. Like all glamour, it seemed a little false, but you couldn't say so without sounding, possibly being, envious. He swaggered. He was able to be snotty to kids a whole level above Allen and Judy. He was able to be snotty to some of the teachers, mostly the ones who taught stenography or mechanical drawing. He dressed better than almost anybody who wasn't an outright homo, and a cloud of Old Spice followed him down the halls, just like it did for his dad. "Like his dad" was the key, actually, for day by day Vince Jr. was more like Vince Sr. Physically, he was almost there. He just needed to put on a few muscle-y inches. He was even developing the doubtful, accusatory squint that drew thick lines back from his father's eyes.

Used to be you never saw Coach and Vince in the hall together. Now you did. Coach sometimes ate lunch with us in the dining hall, spooning in the same brown slop Mrs. Wirtz dolloped onto every plate as it passed. You could watch Coach watching his son, like a scientist observing some new behavior he didn't yet know how to classify.

Vince and I still double and triple dated, but if it was a triple, now, it was with some other guy on the squad filling the place Tilden and his girl used to fill. Tilden's discovery that he was a brain lessened his interest in football, and Coach could no longer hold things like scholarships over his head. He had his own scholarship and he'd never have to touch a pig skin again if he didn't want to. If Coach didn't have some power over you, he wasn't interested, and so Tilden drifted to the side—I have to admit for me too, a little. There are just so many hours in a day.

But Tilden got whole evenings and nights to himself when he'd come over on Friday and just stay as deep into Saturday as he wanted. Andy was about to be his brother-in-law, so it was all about the drawing of the family ties tighter. He'd sleep in the bunks with me, and we'd talk until the dark of morning, sleep until Mom shouted from downstairs that we'd better come to breakfast or we weren't getting any. We seldom mentioned Glen, though he was the subtext to many of our thoughts. He was the one of us who had been claimed by fate. In our superstition—derived from the myth of the Falls—that meant that the rest of us could breathe easy, at least for a little while.

"Do you miss him?" Tilden said. I knew whom he meant.

We'd built a fire in the fireplace (Tilden had to reach up in there and fiddle with the flue to make it draw right, and there was still a little soot on his forehead). I said, "Not as much as I should. It's as though he was—"

"Vince's."

"Yeah."

"You were Vince's for a while."

"Not in the same way."

Tilden waited for me to elaborate. I didn't. Tilden poked a stick into the coals so they sent up a shower of gold. He said, "I don't think he ran away."

"I know you don't. Everybody else does."

"Sherry doesn't."

"What do you mean 'Sherry doesn't'? When have you been talking to Sherry?"

"All the time, man. We go to the same school."

I tamped down the ludicrous spike of jealousy that had just rammed up through my gut. I managed a very neutral, "Oh?"

"We both think he went down into the gorge. Under the Falls."

"You think he's dead."

"I didn't say that."

"You think he *lived* there?"

"I didn't say that."

I let silence grow. I almost asked him what he meant by that—it sounded like the beginning of a ghost story—but I knew. I remembered those days, maybe a week or two, when Glen felt pending in a way I can't explain. And then it was over, like the ringing of a bell at the closing of a class. I knew what he meant.

"Tilden, they looked down there. In the gorge. The cops. Andy too."

"I know. I know. Still."

Tilden would come over to my bed so he could be the little spoon. This used to irk me—him getting all the heat and protection, as usual—but after a while it seemed right. It would have been awkward otherwise.

We took the Region that year, and though we couldn't avoid being clobbered by the big Piedmont and Downstate schools, we won whatever was winnable within our mountain purlieu. Coach's stock could hardly be any higher, and we all caught a little of that radiance. We could have done better, though. We could have won with more honor. Vince had his scholarship to UT, and what had once been solid technique turned to razzle-dazzle. He ran sometimes when he should have passed. He made sure he started every game, when it had been customary to let the second string quarterback—in this case Huey Schuckman—start at least once so he could say he started on his high school team senior year. Even showing off like that he avoided injury, which was enough of a miracle to make us assume the gods were on his side.

The New Year's party at Carmen's house was the biggest one anybody had heard of. School colors banners hung all over, so it was as much the hundredth victory party as it was an observation of the holidays. Carmen had hired a band from Johnson City, and though they only played the same hits we could have played ourselves on the Victrola, having a live band at a house party was so outré we figured any extremity of behavior would, therefore, be justified. Only the hillbillies outside the town played their own music anymore. We were a little at sea. It was wild in a way even we wild frontiersmen were not used to. Carmen, what with being a transplanted city girl, was ahead of us in terms of social sophistication, and a lot of us felt uncomfortable without being able to put our fingers on why. Carmen's parents were supposed to be chaperoning, but I never laid eyes on them. There was plenty of beer, and white lightning from the secret special suppliers that we all had somewhere and talked of in whispers as though they were veins of silver. You put the white lightning into your lime sherbet punch and you were flying.

Sherry was visiting her people in Mississippi for the holidays, so I went stag, without liking it much. Tilden went stag too, and so we hitched up and made out like we were boyfriends, which confused some, irked others, amused still others, but we didn't care. I was way drunker than Tilden, and I needed him to keep me from slumping to the floor and passing out. As always, he was my good angel, and after midnight and the toasting and kissing (I kissed Carmen hard and long, just to show I could) he dragged me out into the night air. He said, "We're walking home. You'll be alert enough when we get there that you won't have to explain anything to your mom."

A car idled at the curb outside Carmen's house, its parking lights on. Tilden said, "Shit, Arden, did you tell your mom? Did you ask her to come and pick us up?"

I didn't, and she hadn't. It was Andy in the car. He turned on the headlights when he saw us coming. The beams of the headlights went this incredible silver-green in the grass, and it was there we saw the first pearls of gray sleet that entered the darkness in the year's last hour. As Tilden was climbing into the back, the freezing rain came for real, slashing and driven down harder by the lead weight of the sky.

Andy said, "Was that timing or what?"

"So, Andy, did you just happen to appear, or—"

"You can hear the band clear down to the church."

"But how did you know when to—"

"I went through all this myself. I thought you were going to drive, and I'm a cop now and couldn't let that happen. Glad Tilden was with you."

"God, me too. We were making out, you know." I made a smooching sound in Tilden's direction.

Andy said flatly, "Of course you were."

A block from where you turn from Main Street onto Linden, where we lived, we were suddenly engulfed by emergency vehicles. Andy pulled over to let an ambulance scream past him toward the river, with a fire rescue vehicle throbbing in its wake. Nothing much happened in our town, so when it did, it was disturbing, even when the odds were heavy on a false alarm. Andy said, "Only one of those is ours. Must be—something."

Andy started to pull out again when four police cruisers—who knew there were four police cruisers in our part of the world?—set sirens on full and went blasting off in the same direction. Andy did this exaggerated bug-eyed cartoon examination of the street before he pulled out again.

"Should you—"

"I've got the night off," said Andy. "At least until Dadlez calls."

You could tell from his face that Tilden was as happy in Andy's company as I was. But finally my poor friend said, "Andy, it's the best thing in the world to be with you guys on New Year's, but I have to piss so bad."

Andy motioned to one of the lordly red maples Main Street is known for. Every cop car in the county had already screamed past us, so if you were going to piss against a tree on Main Street, this would be the time to do it. Tilden got out, took his piss, and, recognizing the unique opportunity, danced around a little for our benefit with his dick hanging out the front of his pants.

Refreshed, Tilden was squirming back into the car when sirens blasted back down Main Street, going the opposite direction, heading for police headquarters or Mercy Hospital or somewhere. Another went the other way, or maybe the same one, changing its mind and turning. The sirens were confused and crossing each other in the night. Maybe ice had pulled down power lines up nearer the mountains. The coves were forever going dark and the hillbillies having to light their candles with Bible verses on them and wait it out.

Tilden intended to spend the night, so we all tumbled out onto the sleet in our yard. We shoved each other and laughed our way up the steps into the kitchen. The freezing rain came so hard you could hardly lift your face into it and keep breathing. The kitchen was brightly lit. Harshly, even. Mom stood there with a look on her face. Paper plates from the adult party they'd had were stacked neatly on the counter. A pot of sauerkraut sent its perfume into the air. Mom said, "Andy, the chief called. Somebody is lost in the Gorge."

Tilden said, "Fuck me."

Mom had been making coffee. She began pouring it into Thermoses, adding a Thermos when she saw Tilden.

Dad walked into the room. "Is the car in the drive, Andy?"

"Yes."

"We've got to go. We've got to go down to the river. To help."

"Was it those sirens? Is someone drowned?"

"Yes. I don't know. They think someone is missing. She left a note—Judy. Dale Herman's little girl."

"Muffin?" Tilden said. A smile flickered at the corners of his mouth. Surely it was a hoax. A New Year's prank. I wanted to smile too, but fortunately forced it back. Dad didn't look like he thought it was a joke.

Andy said, "I have to get to—"

Dad interrupted. "We're all going. There aren't enough cops. Even with you, son. The call went out for the men."

The men of the town were mustering to meet calamity, just as in days of yore. It was rather grand, after all.

We piled into the car. Dad followed, plopping heavily down into the driver's seat. Andy handed him the keys. The fact that he didn't speed toward the river frightened us. Maybe there was no more need to hurry.

Riverside Park blazed with flashlights and the beams of cars, a confusing jumble of black and gleam and falling sleet. Coach stood in a ring of light with a look on his face that I couldn't identify. He was holding coffee, but he wasn't drinking it. He had a hood on his slicker, but it hung limp down his back, while his hair flattened and his face gleamed with droplets. People spoke to him and he answered, but he didn't move from that spot. Whether he helped or not, the men needed him, and he seemed to know it. You didn't appreciate how slight he was, really, until he got among the other men.

Chief Dadlez directed the operations. He sent me and Tilden upstream to check if she might be hiding in the little woods with the cement pagoda where kids played all the time. He gave us a flashlight. The pagoda woods were small, even in the dark. The pagoda looked like it was trying to hide under a wet mass of English ivy. Tilden and I knew she wouldn't be there anyway. It was upstream from the bridge, from which any sensible person would jump, if they were going to jump. Maybe Dadlez just didn't want a kid to be the one to find her.

Tilden said, "I keep seeing her going over the Falls."

"Me too. Like that dog."

"Except we aren't there to stop her. Everything that goes into the water here goes into the air there."

"Yes."

"I hope Glen was right about that door at the bottom."

Walking back into the confusion of lights I realized something. Coach Silvano was gazing downstream, but nobody was going downstream. Chief Dadlez had sent no one that direction, the one it was almost 100% certain she had gone, if she had gone into the water at all. It wasn't an oversight. They didn't want to know for sure, just yet. They didn't want to find her. They wanted Judy Herman to come strolling down the road carrying an umbrella, late home from a party, sorry that she had caused so much to-do. At worst, they wanted to find her by the light of day. I walked up to the chief. I hadn't realized he was old and frail, because he didn't look it most of the time when he was bossing people around. I said, "Chief Dadlez, you know we're not going to find her up here."

Dadlez said, "I don't know anything of the like." But you knew he did.

Andy was less doctrinaire about things, and soon he got a group including my dad and Tilden and me moving downstream, sweeping our flashlights over the opaque brown river. If she had sunk we would never see her. We'd have to go all the way to the Falls and hope she snagged on something. Finally most of the party moved west, downstream. Coach carried the coffee cup in front of him like he'd forgotten it was there. It must be half sleet water by now. All of the men had Thermoses. You had to stop to drink out of them, or else you'd slosh scalding coffee onto your face. The milling, raincoated contingent eased forward foot by foot, blasting the mud and the agitated water with rays of light as it went.

Tilden said, "Why is Coach here?"

One of the boys from school—it was hard to tell who under the rain gear—shouted, "Because there wasn't a day in the week he didn't wait at the door to call her 'Muffin' when she came in."

Coach looked like he was just staring off into space, but it was he who shot out his arm and shouted "There!" dropping the cup into the speeding water. Something that was less like water than everything else was bobbing on the near side of the river, snagged on the roots of a clump of willow. In the dark you couldn't see the color, but it was blue. It was Judy's blue raincoat that everyone knew—once they stopped to think about it—and she was still in it. The way the Wyona was treating her, it almost looked like she was alive, lifted up by the waters, then settled gently down. Maybe she was alive, those last few moments. But she was gone by the time we got her to shore. Coach was the one who waded into the furious freezing river—it was up to his chest most of the time—and grabbed the coat. He could get her to solid ground, but he couldn't carry her through the close trees and the underbrush. He was howling down there in the blackness until we got there to help. I'd never heard such a sound from any man, and never expected it from Coach. Was it fear or grief? You couldn't tell from his face. When he thrashed back up on shore, carrying the body with four others, his face was back to a cipher, cruel and handsome in the swiveling flashlights.

Poor Muffin. Everyone went to her funeral. Some of the guys from the team couldn't stop giggling and elbowing one another in the ribs. Mom said it was nervousness, how uncomfortable people, especially the young, were around death. I hoped so.

XI

Mrs. Herman, Judy's mother, appeared at assembly one morning to thank us for our kindness toward her daughter. She wore one of those hats where the pheasant feather curves all the way around to the back. Anyone with a straw of conscience bent over in his seat in an attitude of mortification. Thank God the posture could be taken for reverence. You focused on the feather because otherwise you'd be sick. We had not been kind to her daughter. Some of us had been neutral, harmless, as it were, but search as we might we could not find one person who had actually been her friend. Some of us scanned Mrs. Herman's face for the scalding irony that should have been there. Not a trace. The woman was straightforward as a wife on a radio play.

". . . and I know all is in God's hands, and that you will not blame yourself for the terrible thing that happened. All ways are mysterious, and none more so than the ways of youth." She was eloquent, really, her wide brow clear under pale brown hair. She looked like her daughter, and maybe her daughter's skin would have cleared and she would have grown up to be a handsome woman.

Judy and her mother had been working on a project together, which she had completed alone and meant to present to the school as a gift and memorial. It was a quilt of the North Carolina flag. She held it by the top edge and let it unroll toward the floor. The gasp from some of the girls was genuine. It was quite lovely. And then she said, "Will one of Judy's special friends come down and accept this gift on behalf of Rickenbacker High?" The smile on her face could have lit a campfire. I have lived life not devoid of embarrassment, but that moment was the worst of all. Agonizing. Excruciating. But in less time than it probably seemed, someone was moving down the aisle. It was Sherry. Of course it was Sherry, beaming a smile back to match Mrs. Herman's. God had given me the best girl in the world. This time she saved us all. Sherry took one side of the quilt and motioned for Mrs. Herman to take the other, and they held it up before us all. When Sherry nodded we knew we were meant to applaud.

The quilt went up in the lobby opposite the dining hall, where everybody would see it all the time. It hung there in lone splendor for a while, but then Mrs. Herman began to do an odd thing. She began to gather remnants and remembrances of all the Rickenbacker kids (and those who'd gone to Borderland High before the name was changed) who had died before they graduated. She got the principal to get the janitor to set up a cabinet like a trophy cabinet, and into the cabinet went sad little tokens of lives cut short: Chancel Beatty's gym shirt from the day he collapsed at recess and could not be revived; Clarence Burden's varsity letter; Timmy Hanson's ball cap; Anita Coleman's bracelet with the single cultured pearl hanging like a dewdrop. When long-grieving relatives heard of the project, they sent items and pictures in tarnished brass frames. The collection grew. Kids die of all sorts of things, but what was creepy was how many of us had died on the Falls or in the gorge. One in every generation, at least, just as the local wisdom prophesied. The principal turned his countenance against it, saying it was "morbid" and that youth is a time not to think about such things (he'd evidently forgotten about the War, just two years in the past), but we overruled him by simply standing in the lobby and looking our fill, quiet for once, contemplative. When I dropped by Glen's parents' house to see if they had a token of his they'd like to enshrine, it was the first time I realized they were gone, slipping away between one day and another with a word, so far as I knew, to no one.

Mrs. Herman attended graduation. She stood up and received applause when her daughter's name was called and after it the words, "In memoriam." We had forgotten the tormented Judy-mouse haunting the halls, and remembered her as her mother did, the belle of the ball. Maybe that had been Mom's goal all along.

And then we were high school graduates. Dad gave me two weeks to lounge around in the June sun before I joined him in the hardware store. I took two days. He said nothing. He handed me a brand new apron he had been saving for the moment. I thought how Mom and Dad had been with me all the time, through everything, unvarying, unwavering, root and stone, and I had to turn my face away for a minute.

It's not that Sherry never said she intended to become a teacher, nor is it that I didn't take her seriously. It's that I didn't know exactly what becoming a teacher involved. I knew Nancy McWhirter had gone to college, but she was an outsider, and I assumed that if you were an outsider you had to go to college, but if you were a local as clearly brilliant as Sherry you just moved right in to a vacant position at the school. No, I didn't assume that. I gave it no thought at all. I talked from time to time about being this or that—a pilot or a diver or a cop like Andy, but I had no real ambition or desire to take it beyond talk. Sherry talked about being a teacher in the very same tone, and yet she damn well meant to be exactly that. That Sherry would have to choose between me and a profession never crossed my mind, and that she would not choose me was not even a remote possibility. Yet, that's what happened. She wouldn't have said it this way. She would say that she just asked me to wait a little while she finished her course work in Cullowhee. I am one of those people who takes a setback for defeat. I sobbed myself to sleep because my time with Sherry was over and I wanted no one else. One minute after noon is night.

She suggested I come along and get a college degree. With her. Leave my home and move . . . to a strange mountain beside a strange river. I couldn't get my head around that. I intended from my first consciousness to work with my dad in the Summers Family Feed and Hardware, take it over some day, and I could no more have deviated from that than flown to the moon. Sherry somehow took her refusal to stay with me and mine to go with her as equivalent. I didn't get that at all.

She invited me to visit her at Western for Homecoming, and I did, and we had a good time (she even agreed to leave the dance and make out in her room after about an hour of stupid big-band rumbas), so the pain of rejection began to soften. My suspicion that she was humoring me until she could break away clean lessened, and my fear that she would think me a rube after hanging out with philosophers and mathematicians grew. There was no pleasing me. I would be content relationship-wise only when we were married. I told her this and she said, "You mean, only when you own me." She was smiling, so I didn't know whether she was serious.

I did sort of mean that, but I intended for her to own me too.

That was the bad after graduation. The good was that I was, as I always suspected I would be, happy as a pig in shit helping Dad run the store. I adored measuring out the nails and matching the bolts and jamming the big scoops into the bins of seed and setting up the lighted pens for the baby chicks at the end of winter. I ran toward the people coming to the door, desiring to hear what they wanted, desiring to feel myself getting it for them. I made keys and repaired engines and sharpened blades and, after a while, chose what bulbs to get in for the local gardeners in October. I stopped ordering hammer X because hammer Y was a better value, and I trusted myself to know the difference. Dad was so proud he didn't know where to look. At the business end, I was more up to date than he was, having taken the two business courses offered at the high school. But Dad was way better at talking to the people. I wanted to know what they needed and how I could get it to them. Dad wanted to know how the pig barn was holding up, and was Granny still poorly, and how were those feed bins working? I could do three customers to his every one, but after a while I learned that was not the point. I learned that you could, if you wanted to, retain obscure details of people's lives and repeat them back to them when they came into the store next time, and that this would make them happy. Some called me by my dad's name, as though there would be no interruption from one generation to another. This made me proud.

So, that's the bad and the good. The weird was Vince. UT was not that far away, and yet, after the first few weeks of fall practice, we heard nary a word from or about him. I called him at the university, but could never quite get connected. The university switchboard operator started saying he wasn't there, but I knew better. He was the star of their football team. I ran into Coach in the grocery store and tried to ask him about his son, but I got a wave of the hand to part me from him as though I had bad breath. Maybe I did. I decided to let that pass. But something about the exchange made me determined to get news of my best friend, so I strolled to the Silvano house when I knew Coach would be at school. I didn't even need to knock. Mrs. Silvano was sitting on the top step of the front porch with a cigarette in her hand at the end of an extended arm resting on her left knee the whole duration of my approach down the sidewalk, so whether she were actually smoking it or not, I didn't know. Beside her was a tumbler of clear brown liquid which she moved behind her into semi-concealment when she realized I was coming up her walk.

"Mrs. Silvano!"

"Hello there. If you're the paper boy you'll have to come back when—"

"It's Arden Summers. Remember? Vince's friend?"

She stared like she thought I was lying. "It's the middle of the day . . . well, of course you've graduated, haven't you?"

"Yes ma'am. Same year as Vince."

"Well, isn't that nice?" She drew the cigarette to her lips but did not quite take a drag on it before she let her arm fall again. That cigarette must have weighed a ton. Mrs. Silvano was thin and angular in a fashionable way. She was dressed pretty well for somebody just hanging around the house in the middle of the day. One leg was crossed over the other all ladylike, enabling a posture whereby she could support that cigarette on one knee.

"Arden, Arden," she said. "Aren't you in college? I think one of Vince's friends is down at Duke."

"That's Tilden, ma'am."

"He was a good boy. He playing ball?"

"No ma'am. He is studying physics."

"Physics!" She drew the word out as though it were the most amazing concept ever encountered. "You? You're still playing ball, I hope. Vincent loves his boys so much."

"I'm working at my dad's store."

"Of course you are. HARD-WARE." The word made her laugh. She laughed a little throaty laugh, paused, and then laughed again at a rather jarring volume. I didn't know what to do. I waited for it to be over.

"Things going OK for you?"

"Peachy." I waited for a moment. She said, "Harris."

"That's my dad."

"I know. I just . . . I just got a clear image of him. Like he was sending me a message or something. You don't favor him much. "

"I look more like my mom."

"Don't remember her." She lifted the cigarette again, and this time she took a long drag, held it, blew a blue stream of smoke into the air. "It's your dad I remember. Harris. We grew up together. All of us. Oh, I remember Harris Summers." She laughed as she had over "hardware," first perfunctory, then chaotic. After the laugh she had a coughing fit. I waited for it to be over. I thought about asking what the hell she meant, but I remembered one of life's rules is not to ask questions you don't want the answers to.

When she seemed to be recovered I said, "Well, I wondered. I haven't heard from Vince . . . and . . . I wondered . . . if I could get his school address from you. He's been so mysterious! I'm my own boss now . . . don't tell my dad I said that . . . and I wanted to drive up . . . maybe pay him a visit . . . me and Sherry . . . if I could . . ."

The look on her face was odd, as if there were a whole array of things to be said and she had to choose but one of them. She took another drag of the cigarette, coughed once, hard and sharp. Then she said, "No. I don't think that would be a very good idea at all."

Sherry didn't take much convincing, though we had to wait until she could take a long weekend. She hitched a ride with a girlfriend up from Cullowhee, then we were off to Knoxville with some little sandwiches her mother had made, like the kind you have at weddings, with olives and cream cheese and weird stuff in them. If we ever got married it was going to be a mixed marriage, bologna and white bread on one side, tiny ethnic smelly cheesy assortments cut into shapes on the other. I loved her anyway.

We'd set aside a whole weekend to spend with Vince. We didn't need it. Vince was not at UT, just like the switchboard operator had said. He got there, he practiced a few weeks with the team, looked good. Then he started getting queer. This is the evaluation of his roommate, a second-year linebacker who weighed about three hundred pounds: "queer."

Sherry said, "How do you mean 'queer'?"

Girls were not allowed in the dorms, so we stood in the lobby, catching the taint of male sweat subliming from the interior. Freddy the Linebacker said, "You know. Crybaby.

Homesick, I guess. Something like that. He picked a fight with me and I didn't say anything. He picked a fight with Coach and that was the end of it."

"He fought his dad?"

I hadn't remembered where I was. Freddy's uncomprehending stare brought me back to the present.

"You take a swing at one of the coaches and there's just no place for you. He spent a night in jail."

"He spent—"

"Yeah. Coach is big on lesson-teaching. He was flunking out anyway."

"Your coach was flunking out?"

"*Silvano* was. Went to class maybe once."

I didn't know where to take it from there. We chit-chatted about expectations for the UT team that year and whatnot. Freddy revealed that he wanted to be a business major, but there was some test he had to take first, and wouldn't I take it for him because nobody knew me there. I said I would and gave him an imaginary address to write to when the time neared. Sherry said she was worried by how my deviousness had become almost reflexive.

I said, "It's because I'm hungry."

"You ate enough of those sandwiches."

"It's not possible to eat enough of those sandwiches."

About ten miles below Knoxville, Sherry said, "That's not what you expected to hear, is it?"

"Nope. I thought Vince was just—"

"You thought he was the General MacArthur of college football now and had no time for his small town friends anymore."

"Yes. I wish it had been that."

About twenty miles below Knoxville, Sherry said, "Tell me something."

"Yeah?"

"Did you hear what he called you?"

"Who? The linebacker? I never told him my name."

"I know. He called you Glen. Twice."

Some time later I did get the long-awaited call from Vince. His voice sounded tired and young, as though he'd been growing backwards away from us. I watched a gang of crows feeding on something in the backyard while I talked to him. The two things seemed related in a way I can't describe.

"Ardo."

"Man, where the hell have you been?"

"Oh . . . man. A long story. Just let me . . . I just want to hear the sound of your voice."

When I realized that was exactly what he meant, I talked, about Sherry, about the high school, about the town, about the new gizmos Dad had gotten into the store and relied on me to figure out. One was the first TV anybody had in our town, for sale to anyone who had the money, with me to explain and assemble and maybe repair a little. Vince was not forthcoming about his own life, except to tell me where he was calling from. In a time when you actually paid for long distance, the remoteness of a call could be a measure of friendship, and I boasted to Sherry that my best friend had plunked down cash to phone me from St. Louis.

"What's in St. Louis?"

"Glen."

I don't know. Maybe he went looking for Glen. It was something you could never know for sure. Connections were bad in the mountains. Vince's voice on the line came and went like a ghost . . . twice, three times . . . and then it stopped.

The high school was the big thing in our town, so its news was our news. You could read in the *Watauga Advertiser* of the opening preparations for the celebration people were planning to honor Coach's twentieth anniversary. He'd coached only sixteen years, but they counted the four years he played under Coach Andonian and ignored the four intervening years he'd spent at Auburn. Chairwomen were chosen for this and that committee. Funds were solicited. Pledges were pledged. It was still a long way off, so I decided not to pay that much attention, though my alumnus invitation to the big banquet arrived almost immediately—in the hope, I suppose, that I would help or contribute money. I'd be there for sure. I could idolize Coach with greater purity now that I wasn't around him every day.

The other source of excitement was the matter of the school mascot. School mascots had not been common in our part of the world. You were known by your town (in a place where most towns had only one high school) or your colors, but one by one the regional schools began to call themselves the Catamounts or the Spartans or what have you. I guess they picked this up from the North. Anyhow, our being Eddie Rickenbacker High, "The Aces" won hands-down in a single ballot. All this was set up to happen at the same time: the assumption of a nickname, the unfurling of all the new banners and modeling of all the new uniforms, and the honoring of the winningest coach in our corner of the world. Little towns like ours are asleep most of the time, but when we wake, we are relentless.

I walked into the store and saw, on a poster the size of a mattress, that Summers Family Feed and Hardware was a main sponsor of Coach's big do. Dad is not a talker, so it took me a while to figure out why he was so enthused about this. I knew he and Coach had been buddies as Vince and I were, but you never attribute the same keenness of emotion to other generations as you do to your own. Vince Jr. and I have been buddies since before we remember. Dad has pictures of us playing together in my grandpa's backyard, under the colossal sweet gum, from when we looked pretty much alike, as babies do. The sweet gum tree had remained unchanged from the time when somebody took a photo of my dad and Vince's dad in the very same spot, looking like us, looking like their sons would a quarter century later, all Marine-cut heads and ears and white T-shirts. The boys are a little older in my dad's picture, and holding onto things that help to explain their lives. Vince's dad is holding a football, as he was going to pretty much forever after. My dad was holding onto a book. You can read the title of the book through the fingers of his chubby little hand. The book is *The Official Boy Scout Book of Home Repairs*. Those two objects summarized what their lives would become. You'd think only in a movie would one turn out to be the high school football coach and the other the owner of the town hardware store, but that is exactly what happened. Copies of that photo endured in both houses, one on our kitchen wall, one in the Silvano hallway, as if it had been a kind of diploma, or a contract sealing a partnership, whatever came after. The point is Dad and Coach were friends from youth, when friendship first meant something. Men of that generation sometimes waited a good while for a means to show love that would abash neither party.

Many things became clear when that relationship became clear: how Dad would not allow me to call Coach a shithead even when he was; how Dad would once in a while reach out and caress Vinny in a way that puzzled me—in the sense of making me absurdly jealous—until I realized that for a moment Dad was not seeing my friend, but his own twenty years before; how Dad was never surprised when I told him about our adventures at the Falls or in the gorge of the Wyona, was never as worried as I expected him to be. This dismayed me a little, wondering why he wasn't more protective of his precious second son. At some point I must have realized that he and Vince Silvano Sr. had been there in their time, watched the swifts in the tornado of their evening descent, heard the water running under the bent moon, had done what all their sons would do a generation before they did it. It was kind of beautiful not to have invented anything, really, but to have carried on a tradition older than any one person in the world. I was glad to be where I was. Every night until dead winter the swifts sank into the mountain and the bats beat out of it, and it was like a beating heart by which all things were made alive.

The Sanctified Brotherhood Church Hall was chosen for the banquet. More obvious places, like the school cafeteria, were out because they were in use every day and the sort of preparations the committees planned needed to gather to a greatness untouched. The nine or ten of the Sanctified Brotherhood who remained could probably manage to keep out of the basement for a couple of weeks. Everyone in town had once been Sanctified Brotherhood, and the drafty dark 1816 church took up most of what would have been a city block, had our town been a city. I don't know what the Sanctified Brotherhood believed distinct from what other folks believe, but only that, long before I came into the world, most of them had stopped believing it. Still, it was rich somehow, the church was, and kept going long after there seemed to be no point. Maybe it had kept itself alive so it could host this one last grand to-do.

Stupendous was the achievement of the town ladies, the Boosters and the alumnae and the mothers of current Rickenbacker Aces, in the decorating of the Sanctified Brotherhood basement. That sort of thing was strictly gender-specific, and though men were present to handle the tools, they drilled where the women told them to drill and hammered where the women told them to hammer. The celebration of males in a male activity curiously overflowed with female energy. Walls were covered with brown butcher paper painted with the very mountains that could be seen if one walked out the front door. The paintings were fine, shockingly so, as if years of pent-up artistic energy had come pouring out at this one moment. My dad donated the paint and solvents and brushes and various kinds of adhesive, but the women worked, with their hair tied up in bandanas, floors covered in torn and stained sheets from the laundry room, doors propped open to let the toxic fumes out into the air. Women we had never seen before came to the store to replenish their supplies. They didn't ask advice even once. I didn't understand how they could know what they needed without men around to tell them. I worried that they had been taking their custom elsewhere, but Dad said women had a way of controlling things without themselves being present, and so they never had to go to the hardware store at all if they didn't want to.

Tree limbs got dragged down from the hills, balanced in pails, and covered with paper blossoms intricately folded. Sunday schools and funeral parlors and classrooms were

emptied of chairs and folding tables, which the school jani-
tors set up after hours, rank on rank with the Honoree's Table elevated at Upstage Center, just as in the movies. Florists
in Johnson City and Jonesboro were alerted to be ready on
the fateful day. Uniforms not currently in use got straight-
pinned to the wall, helmets hung from the ceiling by strings
as though they were enormous red fruit. Someone got the
idea to simulate victory bonfires, so those fake fires you put
in cardboard fireplaces at Christmas came out of attics all
over town to make an unseasonal appearance, their pin-
wheel flame-makers turning at various velocities so if you
paid too much attention it would make you sick. Dad and I
and some of the other men repaired, reinforced, suggested,
but the women were in charge.

Mrs. Silvano served as the honorary head of everything,
though she was . . . confused . . . and spent her time waving
her hand vaguely at the decorations and saying how beautiful it all was. It was pretty much done two weeks in advance.
Should the Russkies drop their bomb and the rest of civili-
zation be wiped out, Coach's jubilee could go on as planned
upon our hidden mountain.

Sherry had a few weeks before she went back to her sopho-
more year at Western. My fears about her commitment to
me faded some through the summer as we spent nearly every waking hour together. Tilden had flown overseas for the
summer—Denmark, I think, or someplace where the phys-
icists grew thick—so she was my main company. Even if she
were sick of me, I needed her. I went to her house to watch
her fold invitations and lick stamps. I could have helped her,
but, as I say, the line between the work of men and the work
of women was pretty clear in those days. It also gave me a

rare chance to dominate the conversation, as at least part of the time her tongue was on a stamp or the back of an envelope. She looked at me with her golden eyes over the tops of the envelopes. It was very sexy.

She said, "I know something you don't know."

"Probably."

"Wanna guess?"

"French."

"Besides that."

I grabbed at the envelope now in process, thinking it was something to do with that. She pulled it away and said, "No, it's not that. I know where Vince is."

"So do I."

"You think you do. I have the address. I already sent him his invitation."

"Where?"

"Gallipolis."

"What the hell is Gallipolis?"

"It's a little town in Ohio. The address is a high school. Arden, I think he's coaching."

I said, "God, that's wonderful," but I meant about the coaching. To be in Gallipolis, Ohio seemed, on the other hand, sad almost beyond expression.

XII

Though the Event was but one day, one evening and one night, people arrived for it from the far corners of the world, and those who didn't drive had to be picked up at bus stations in Asheville and Johnson City. War shortages remained an undimmed memory, and in some place gas went for as high as twenty cents a gallon. Fair summer weather turned stormy and temperamental as the day approached, but we were so well prepared that every outdoor venue had an indoor exigency, and even if the power went out, my dad had stacked boxes of candles in the Sanctified Brotherhood basement, and it would be more romantic than if the lights stayed on. The very night before, the rain intensified, hard and ceaseless. Just as the deluge hit a pitch of fervor and endurance, I received a call to pick someone up at the Johnson City bus station. I wasn't told who, and didn't ask. I watched the wipers and the wind rearrange the waves on the windshield for a miserable hour. When I got to the station I saw it was Vince.

There were two others who needed a ride back in the Summers Hardware van. One was Coach's old coach from Auburn, whose eyesight had gotten so bad he couldn't drive (though evidently he still coached) and the other was a guy from the Rickenbacker varsity a few years before us who had gotten really roly-poly in that time, and kept worrying aloud if Coach would think he was fat. "Of course he will," nobody said, "you *are* fat." I didn't care about them. I hugged Vince so hard we had to go back inside the station so I could hug my fill without drowning anybody. Vince was thin and haunted, but the waif look worked for him, and he was, to my mind, more beautiful to look at than anybody I knew. I couldn't even make an exception for Sherry. Sherry was too healthy to stab you in the heart like that. The rain covered up the tears in my eyes, and my ardor made Vince laugh a little, like he did in the old days. Of course he got the invitation. Of course he would come. Of course he would be there. Only one Rickenbacker player had come even close to the renown of Vince Silvano Sr., and that was Vince Silvano Jr. Of course he was there. How could his father stand before us all without his son? The star was re-ascendant.

I said, "Tilden drove in this morning."

"It'll be great to see him."

"How are those Ohio boys?"

"Big. Something cramps you up here in the mountains. You can't spread out. They're big, Vince, and they play hard."

"We played hard."

"Yes. We did."

Vince and his dad's old coach had a conversation about "playing hard" and the different things that means to different people. Then I said:

"So, when you coming home?"

Instead of the guffaw I expected, he said, "I've been giving that a lot of thought."

"So what the hell kind of town is Gallipolis?"

"Just like this one. Only really, really different." Vince chuckled at his own joke. The fat guy let out a ringing snort, just to show he was in the conversation.

"What does it mean? The name?"

"Oh, Chicken City or something. I forget."

When I tried to make further fun of Gallipolis, he said, "Yeah, but it has a river that makes the Wyona look like someone pissing on a sidewalk."

By the time we crossed the Wyona into town, it no longer looked like piss on a sidewalk, or like itself at all, but a twisty yellow dragon roaring and bumping its head against the bottom of the bridge. The willows that were normally its edge shuddered and swayed in the midst of it.

I dropped the other riders at Maggie's B&B. I stopped by Tilden's to pick him up, so when I got to the high school it was the three of us again. I was so goddamn happy. It was possible Vince would be perturbed by the step backwards in time, but he wasn't. He smiled. He laughed. He wasn't his old self by any means, but what I was missing was a kind of brilliant cruelty that I thought I could do without.

Rain was in it for the long haul. You open the door and the wind drowned you in one second. It was like breathing underwater.

School had not yet opened for the year, so several special programs were planned for the momentarily gleaming and immaculate halls of Rickenbacker High. The space around the doorways bristled with wet umbrellas, most of them useless in and turned inside out by the fierce wind. Everyone who'd gone to the school remembered that wet floors are slick floors, and whole lines of people felt their way along the walls, locker to locker, to avoid slipping. Just like the olden days. Folks began whispering "hurricane," but reception was so bad the radios could not confirm that. It didn't matter. The girls' glee club sang a medley of Armed Forces songs—which were, in fairness, not totally unlike football songs—and several of the teachers manned their rooms to give visitors a taste of current educational process. The band, washed out of their planned formations of the playing field, tooted and bellowed away in the band room. It was like a day at school, but better, because nobody had to do anything or be anywhere, or get bossed by anyone, until the banquet that night.

Mrs. Herman, lost Judy's sad mother, had prepared a special exhibit in the memorial vitrine. It had occurred to her that for every lost child of whom there was remembrance, there might be two or three who had vanished without a trace, or so long ago that no one grieved for them anymore. So she had taken to poking around along the river bank, and even to lowering herself—somehow—down the stone walls into the gorge, searching for remnants. Most of the stuff you found there was junk, and she knew that. But sometimes you'd come across a rotting wallet or a locket, or a once-treasured object that had obviously not gotten there on its own. These she cleaned and restored, and researched. Sometimes it was possible to determine to whom they had once belonged, but even if you couldn't do that, she treasured them as people treasure the Unknown Soldiers under their white stone up in Washington. In making a monument for the lost ones, Mrs. Herman had made a monument of herself, the town's chief mourner and remembrancer. Everyone recognized her pale trench coat poking amid the reeds or easing itself gingerly down the mossy river boulders. Everyone crowded around to what new things she had found along the Wyona, eager to help with the identification. We boys who had found the Falls and made it part of our lives rather thought that things given to the river should be kept by the river. Still, if we didn't aid her search, we honored it, and if we recognized something (like Glen's *Field Guide to the Ferns* which had disappeared from his backpack and lay hidden between two rocks for ten years before she found it) we told her as much of its story as we could.

The line to the exhibit was long. Folks at the front were taking their time, handling things, talking in whispers. You could hear people back toward the door slipping in the puddles and stopping themselves, or failing to stop themselves, from saying "shit." Thunder rolled overhead so continuously that you paid attention when it stopped or slackened. After one tremendous crash the lights flickered and briefly went out. There was, but for the wind and rain, silence. When the lights came back on everybody laughed. Disaster averted. Tilden had gone to the bathroom, but now he was back, cutting the line to be with us.

"Bad planning."

"What is?"

"Having Coach's wingding on such an awful day."

"Blame the ladies. This is their day."

"They didn't say the right spells."

Tilden had probably always been witty, but we didn't notice it until he was a college man. It was sweet to see him tone it down around Vince, who was clearly fragile in some way neither of us quite understood. No cussing. No name calling. Only the gentlest wisecracks. When we were growing up I thought I was the smart one of the group. To find out different was a relief, actually. Vince had always been the good looking one, the athletic one. I guess that left me the Solid One. The Foundation. That was all right.

We stepped a step closer to the front of the line. Vince said, "Do they blame me?"

"Does who blame you for what?"

He gestured with his shoulder toward Mrs. Herman, hovering over her memorial and under the quilt her ghost daughter and she had made, smiling her almost-old-lady smile, yet an icon of sadness, a smile pasted like a mask on a heart that would never again be whole.

"Shit no," I said, lying. Even I blamed him. He didn't push Judy off the bank, maybe, but—

Tilden leapt in and said, "I hear you're coaching up north."

"Yeah. College didn't work out—"

"You can always try again."

"Yeah, I can try again. I'll come down to Duke. We'll be roomies."

"Hell yes," Tilden grinned.

"School didn't work out. I . . . uhm . . . moved around a little. Someone in Gallipolis had heard of me. Knew somebody who knew somebody, you know."

"Like everything."

"Like everything. They were shorthanded, so they tried me out. I'm doing OK. There's a college over in Marietta. Might try that in a year or so. Might get a teaching degree."

Tilden grinned from ear to ear. "Hey, do you remember Nancy McWhirter? The teaching profession has gone downhill since her—"

Another crash, another flicker of lights. A big knot just ahead of us had apparently looked their fill, and it came our turn. Mrs. Herman had done a really excellent job. The permanent display inside the cabinet honored kids from the school, but around about stood a circle of tables on which she had placed artfully various things she had gathered from the river. When she discovered the owner or the circumstance, she made a file card and laid it beside the item with the information printed in an exquisite old-timey hand. When nothing could be learned, the object sat by itself in eloquent silence. For a while it had been the custom of the town girls to throw a doll off the bridge when they got their first period, the end of childhood and all that. Maybe they still did; I didn't know. But on one table sat a sizeable tangle of dolls, battered and hairless, their painted eyes, when they weren't gone altogether, staring and bewildered. It was hard to take it all in. Some of the people one knew, or had heard of. I was musing on Clarence and Timmy Hansen when I saw Tilden's hand dart toward an object on the next table. I looked at him before I looked at the object. His eyes went wide. I knew from his expression that he wouldn't be able to resist his own colorful vocabulary, and in half a second out of his mouth came, "Motherfucker."

Of course everybody turned to look.

The object was an old knapsack, or small backpack. The buckles and rivets were rusted, and the whole thing was probably ten shades paler than it had been when it was new. But the thing was—I knew it—I recognized it without being able right away to say how. Tilden turned it over in his hand. The back of it was sewn with embroidered patches, some of them still amazingly vivid: Boy Scout patches, a golden fleur-de-lis, a couple of hiking patches, a big one from a dude ranch in the desert. Vince and I hit the same spot at the same moment. We knew that backpack. We could fill out Mrs. Herman's file card for her. It was Glen's.

For a moment I thought, as I had at the bonfire, that the moment might fade harmless and without incident into memory.

But Vince let out a terrible cry. He grabbed the pack from Tilden and covered his face with it. It looked like he was trying to sniff it, but he was using it to cover a countenance contorted with grief.

Oooooooo, he cried, *oooooo ooooooo*.

It was terrible to hear. People backed away from him.

"Vince . . . Vince . . . maybe he just—"

Vince retreated into the hall with the bag. He had no place to get away, to hide from the crowd, but in the corridor he found a corner where he could diminish to just side and shoulders. There he shook like a leaf.

"Vince it's OK. It's—"

"I KNEW WHERE HE WAS, SUMMERS. I KNEW AND I DIDN'T COME FOR HIM. I PROMISED TO COME FOR HIM. I PROMISED TEN THOUSAND TIMES THAT I WOULD NEVER LEAVE HIM. HE WAITED. I DIDN'T COME—"

Tilden on the other side said, deep under his breath, "What the fuck is he talking about?"

"I BETRAYED—"

"You couldn't have known—"

"I DID KNOW, ARDEN. I DID KNOW. I—"

Vince stopped mid-sentence, turned, and with the backpack held to his chest, sprinted for the door. As he opened and vanished through it, the biggest flash of lightning yet shattered the night, as if it had been planned to give Vince a terrific exit.

"Should we go after him?" Tilden said.

"And do what?"

We decided to catch up with Vince at the banquet, after he'd settled down a little. I had a clear picture in my head of Glen standing on the bridge, tossing the pack over, cleansing himself of everything that reeked of us. Vince didn't have to ask if people blamed him for *that*, because to those who remembered (and there weren't that many) there was no one else to blame.

You could smell the fried chicken and creamed peas and cornbread and whatnot heating up in the church kitchen. The peaches arrived late, and I helped carry them from Mr. Porter's truck in big industrial cans, which the rain played like snare drums, which needed only to be opened and the contents slopped over some pale cake and covered with whipped cream to be our traditional festival dessert. Three ladies bent over three mixers making sure there was enough whipped cream.

Sherry saved seats for Tilden and me. Vince had a reserved seat at the head table, with Coach. Sherry thought Coach was an idiot, but she'd done more work on the banquet than anyone else, almost. I didn't know how to ask her about that, whether it was some sense of female community, that when the festival came along everyone pitched in, no matter what, or whether she had done it for me. Coach was my coach, and even though I too thought him an idiot, I loved him. Loving someone and hating him at the same time is very good preparation for the real world.

Sherry's hair was done up in a big swoop with a golden comb in it. It looked very exotic. Beautiful, I thought. I didn't know whether I could tell her it was beautiful with Tilden sitting right there.

The room filled quickly. Those without a reserved place jostled for the best seats available. We all watched for Vince. He'd have to be sopping after being out in the rain, and I'd stopped at home for a change of clothes for him. In the past my clothes would have fit him fine, but now he was so thin maybe my dry ones would look worse than his wet. In came the football players with shoulders so wide that everybody bumped into each and wriggled around for breathing room. Though they went or had gone to my school, some of the bruisers I couldn't remember seeing before, or maybe years ago, before they turned into ox-necked giants. Maybe they didn't take classes, but materialized on the field like so many colossal mushrooms just in time for practice. I had been out for a year and already I too was a stranger.

Joey Thornton, the MVP from a couple of years before, had come back from State for the evening. Joey had been Coach's special favorite that year. Beside Joey sat Nick Pettus, Coach's special favorite from this year. They glared at each other like rival beauties at the opera. Most of us kept Southern time, so we didn't notice when the clock crept past the appointed hour for dinner to be served. When it crept past almost a full hour, we began to notice, and at that moment Coach and his entourage entered. When he was sure all eyes were on him, he pointed to his wife and said, "We were waiting for her." Mrs. Silvano smiled and waved, as though she had been paid a public compliment. Coach looked at once pleased and not. It's hard not to feel good about yourself when a hundred people cheer when you entered the room, but something was pissing him off. Maybe the thing that had made him late. Maybe he'd had it out with Vince.

Coach sat down with the mayor on one side and his wife on the other. Mrs. Silvano's gray dress disappeared into the gray chair as though she had planned it that way. The Principal sat beside the mayor, various dignitaries radiating out from them. Coach looked right surrounded by his boys and his boys' dates and a room full of aftershave-doused Adonises who adored him. Coach beamed down at the crowd with a joy I'd seldom seen on his face before. Something empty in him was almost filled. Something watchful and protective could lie down and sleep for an evening. But still, something felt wrong. When Coach saw me looking, he gestured to me. I got up and ran to his table, taking time to shout "Chicken!" over my shoulder as the server asked for my choice of entrées.

"Summers."

"Yes sir."

"Quite a do, no?"

"You're beaming, sir."

He beamed a little brighter. "I never thought anybody would . . . But, you know, I was wondering—" He reached behind the principal and tapped Vince's empty chair. "I was wondering if you'd seen Vince."

"Yeah. At the school."

"Oh, I guess he's on the way. The weather is so fucked."

"Do you want me to look for him?"

He almost said yes, but the air was full of the sound of plates clinking down in front of guests. "Just let it go for now. He'll be here. I know him."

I'd turned back to my seat when a hand plucked the sleeve of my jacket. I thought it was Coach, but it was Mrs. Silvano. She said, "I'm so glad to see you made it."

"Oh, I wouldn't miss Coach's big day."

"Vinny said he had to go find a friend. I thought he meant you, but here you are."

Her beef roast settled in front of her, and she stared at it as though it were the most melancholy thing in the world. I got back to my seat and lifted a chicken leg to my mouth.

"Was that about Vince?" Sherry asked.

"Yeah. Mrs. says he went looking for his friend. We should have told him we'd meet him here."

"He didn't give us much of a chance," Tilden observed, pushing a mouthful of greens to one side so he could talk.

When we had been allowed to gobble and gab for a decent interval, Principal Auten rose. We knew he was but launching into the program that Sherry had prepared. There was a show on the radio called *This Is Your Life*, and Sherry had copied that for Coach, making sure all sorts of people would be there to embarrass him in loving ways. I shushed the bruisers at the table so we could listen. The principal stuck to Sherry's script, pretty much. It was clever. It was funny without wounding. When he realized what was going to happen, Coach's face tightened a little, but as he became assured it was all going to be in good—and for the most part already commonly known—fun, he relaxed. Waves of guffaws washed in from the corners of the room. People mentioned in the script blushed as the whole room turned to find them in the crowd.

"... and we all remember the time when ..."

"... and we're especially glad to have Joseph Thornton back among us, because he will recall more than anybody..."

"... it must have been a tremendous relief to Mrs. Silvano when finally ..."

Laughter came and went, with extended *aaaaah*'s when something tender or sentimental was said. Peach drenched white cake levitated in on the quiet feet of the servers as the Principal joked and jibed. Dessert appearing in the midst of laugher at somebody else's expense—if that isn't the perfect world, what is? Everyone pretty much had their say, those who loved Coach and those who had to pretend they did. It's amazing how mellow and dreamy a room can get even without a drop of alcohol. Good Christian people.

The last miracle was that the cloudburst let up for half an hour while we tried to get into our cars and get home. We barely got the door closed before it started again.

Tilden said, "Fucking Vinny missed the whole show."

Home we went, all of us clustered around the kitchen table rehashing the banquet, at least, of the decade. *Tic tic tic* went the mantel clock. After a while I read Dad's tells concerning how, even though he loved chatting with Tilden and Sherry and me, he was about to sign out for the night. The rain hit the roof so hard I wondered if any of us would be able to sleep. All that sugar in the peach cake would help some. The phone rang. Mom answered. She was being a little passive-aggressive, and I barely heard her "It's for you," sneaking in from the kitchen. I ran and picked up the receiver.

"Hello?"

"Arden? Is this Arden?

"Yes it is."

"This is Maria."

"Maria—?"

"Mrs. Silvano."

"Oh, yes ma'am. What can I do for you?" I was very courteous, but my heart was in my throat. Mrs. Silvano had never called our house, ever. Her voice sounded tired and distant. It did not, however, sound particularly drunk.

"I was just wondering. Vinny is . . . well I was wondering if he was over at your house."

"No ma'am. He's not."

"Oh . . . OK . . . it's just . . ."

"It's just what?"

"He's not here. He's not been here all night. I'm afraid he's out there in the storm."

I'd never heard anything sadder than Maria Silvano's voice saying of her only son, "He's out there in the storm."

When I said, "We'll find him," I looked up to notice everyone was in the kitchen standing around me.

Sherry said, "Vinny?"

"Yes."

Mom said, "That boy—"

Sherry said, "What did his mom say to you again?"

"Just now?"

"No, at the banquet."

"She said he said he was going to look for his friend. But we were already—"

Truth struck everyone in the room at exactly the same second. He didn't mean me. He didn't mean Tilden. He meant Glen.

I set the phone down, picked it up again, commenced dialing.

Mom said, "Didn't that boy go to St. Louis? Or somewhere like that?"

But I knew, at that second, as I had not allowed myself to imagine before, that Glen had not gone to St. Louis or anywhere else. Vince knew all along. Glen had gone to the Falls.

XIII

Tilden borrowed some of my old climbing clothes and an extra slicker. Dad pulled on his black boots, as every man in the town over the age of thirteen might well have been doing right then. Sherry drove home and back again with her slicker on and her yellow middle school boots with the floppy buckles. When the door opened she took only the merest step in. She stood where the stream of water from her coat would go mostly outside. She said, "Well, aren't we going?"

Dad filled his pockets and Tilden's with extra flashlight batteries and lengths of rope. Mom and Sherry huddled over in the corner talking in whispers about whatever it is women talk about at such a time. We were all moving in slow motion. Anxiety added weight to everything. We were almost ready when a whirl of red came to the driveway, like quiet lightning. It wasn't lightning. We knew what it was.

Chief Dadlez was old, but he learned new tricks when he needed to. He probably felt unwelcome in the Summers house, under the circumstances, so he sent two deputies, one a kid Andy went to school with, a few years older, one a cop from Ohio who had moved south for a rest from big-city violence. I don't think he was getting that rest tonight.

The old pro came in first. They were dripping wet, so they huddled together by the door so as little water would get in as possible. We were all in the kitchen anyway, so that was fine.

My mom said, "Coffee?"

Both of them accepted coffee, and held the cups out front in their two hands a second as though they had to inhale the vapors before they could speak. The old pro said, "You all seem to be going somewhere. Or getting back."

Dad said, "One of ours is missing. We thought we'd try some likely spots."

The old pro said, "Do you think maybe you should let the police handle that?" Over his shoulder the kid, Andy's classmate, winced. The older guy had brought some of his city ways with him, and they weren't working particularly well that night.

The kid tried to say, "What we mean is—"

Dad interrupted, "Oh, we know what you mean. Figure there can't be too much help in a situation like this, is all."

The pro was not learning fast. He said, "Yeah, but if we spend all night getting in each other's way—"

Dad interrupted again. "I wonder who it is looking for the boy with you in here jawing to us."

The old pro shot Dad a look that was meant to be a threat, but didn't come off that way. Andy's buddy tried again.

"Oh, Dadlez has things under way. Andy's already out there with a search party. I guess you figured that. But we wondered if there were . . . you know . . . places we should be sure to look . . . things the boy might have said to you that would indicate . . ."

"Vincent," Sherry said, "His name is Vincent. Vinny. If he had said anything like that I bet we would have phoned it in like greased lightning."

The two cops looked uncomfortable. I felt sorry for them. Dadlez had sent them to put the fear of God into us, and keep us out of his way, without warning them what they were up against. They finished their coffee in perfect unison and turned to the door. The young one said, "Well, if you think of anything, I know you'll—"

"We sure will."

The young cop let his partner exit, then stopped dead, looking at Dad. "You're Andy's dad, aren't you?"

"Yes sir."

"I'm sure glad he's with us. I surely am. He is the one all of us think of first at a time like this."

Dad beamed at the kid's back as he disappeared out into the storm.

Wherever Dad and the adults would go, we would go to the Falls. We knew that, separately, from the first moment, and as we came together, one by one, the truth of it didn't have to be spoken. It was a complicated moment. If the cops didn't know about the Falls, then they weren't meant to. Worse still was another thought. Suppose we said, "Try the Falls," and Vince was there, broken on the stones as Clarence had been, a sad pale object in a barrage of cop flashlights? Then it would be over. Then there would not be even an hour or a few moments of hope. It would be finished. But there was something more. The Falls was sacred ground. If Vinny were there, he would not want to be found by just anybody. Tilden and Sherry and I would find him ourselves. We knew without a word among us that this was how it would have to go down.

Tilden said, "What did Vinny say to you?"

"That he knew where Glen was. Always had. But he didn't go to him. He was torn up because he didn't go to him."

A tear formed at the bottom of Sherry's beautiful eye. She said, "I'm afraid he's going to him now."

Tilden said, "Mother of all fuck," in a way so gentle it sounded like a benediction.

We buckled the last buckle, tied the last string. We waited for the cop car to disappear completely. Three or four of the neighborhood men called for Dad. He got up and went to the door, looking over his shoulder at Tilden and me.

"You boys ain't coming with us, are you?"

We shook our heads. He understood.

As Dad tromped away into the raging night, it dawned on us that the neighborhood men had parked in our drive, boxing my car in, and Sherry's too. Sherry said, "Bikes, then."

Mom heard us. She said, "There will be no riding of bikes on a night like this. Why, one gust of that wind—" It sounded like she was out to thwart us, but if you watched carefully, it was a different story. Mom was tying on her rain hat. She was digging her keys out of her purse. She was going to drive us.

Tilden said, "Mrs. Summers, if you could just take 414 up to—"

"I know where you're going."

Mom left the light on, the door open, the coffee singing in the percolator. People were used to coming to our house for coffee in times of disaster, and she saw to it that they still could.

The rain slackened as she drove, even stopping for the space of a few minutes from time to time. The moon tried to break through the flying wrack of midnight blue clouds. Away off over the Smokies, lightning flashed blue and white-gold and the rumble of it shook the road under our tires.

Mom skidded to a stop in the pitch-black parking lot. It was disorienting to be there in the dark and rain. We were in a desperate hurry, so everything took longer. Our clothes caught on things when we tried to exit the car. The trunk lid stuck and I had to open it with a flying kick. We looked for our flashlights, missed them, thought we left them behind, then found them in pockets where we had already looked. Curtains of rain swept the pavement, though whether new rain or wet blown from the trees by the big wind we didn't know. Mom said, "You know why everything is going wrong?"

"No, why?"

"Because you're in a hurry. You know why you're in a hurry?"

"No, why?"

"Because you know Vince is still alive. You know there is reason to hurry."

I thought of the night we searched for Judy Herman in the same kind of downpour. No one was in a hurry. We were men moving in dreams, or in lead, or in an old movie where they can't get the speed right. Yes. We knew Vinny Silvano was alive.

We asked Mom to stay in the parking lot, so she could be seen if anybody passed. We might need help by then. We had no idea what a storm like that would do to the gorge, where the paths would be, what trees would block them, what streams submerge them. If we didn't come out after a time, she would have to go for help.

"It's a full tank," she said, "I'll keep the engine running. I'll keep the lights on."

We made for absolute darkness with the blaze of Mom's headlights at our back. That made it harder, actually, harder to acclimate to the dark, but we wouldn't have done without it. We walked along the beams of light as if we were pearls and it the string.

The ground fell about five feet into utter black. The headlights shot over our heads into the trees. Sherry yelled over the sound of many waters, "Try it without the flashlights!" With flashlights you see only what the lights sees, missing things along the path, things at distance. For Vinny or any sign of him to be right along the path lay beyond the realm of hope.

It took surprisingly little time to learn to see in the dark. Glisten and utter blackness alternated. Light came from somewhere, though we couldn't figure it out exactly. Flashes of lightning came and went, but between them an ambient gleam allowed us to proceed without moon or stars. I took the lead. I felt along the rock wall until pretty certain we were headed the right way. At least the position of the river was never in doubt. It roared and thundered to our left sometimes and sometimes directly before. Every now and then sounded a louder noise, of a tree hitting rock, or a stone easing off its shelf into the torrent. We were astonished that any sound could be louder than the sound of a million gallons of plunging water. I led us to the vantage point from which, long ago, the three of us had first descended, it being the likeliest route for a drop into the gorge. Unless, of course, one meant to jump. You could communicate only by pressing your mouth against the other's ear and shouting. I pressed my mouth against Tilden's ear and said, "We have to go down."

Tilden backed away. Maybe he didn't hear me. I pressed my mouth against Sherry's ear and shouted, "We have to go down!"

She shouted back, "Yes, yes we do!"

Discussion proved impossible, so it was well we were all thinking the same thing: Vinny would have gone into the gorge. He would have sought the door open at the bottom of the river. If we could climb down in this downpour, it meant he could have too.

I leaned over the stone parapet and aimed my flashlight. The beam was startling after the walk in the darkness, startling and yearning and beautiful. Its light struck the crest of the river as it pushed up over the lip of the pool into a great wave before the plunge down. The river shone slimy brown in the lamplight, huge and cresting, like a breaker of the sea. If you watched even for a few seconds you saw debris, some of it recognizable, hurl with the water into nothingness, trunks and brush and trash, sometimes whole trees with their branches shivering in the dark, stalling here and there, snagged on rocks, building up a mass of the river behind them, until irresistible force broke it free and it sailed out and over into the darkness, sometimes large enough to crash at the bottom with a sound to top the blast of the flood.

Tilden shouted, "Vince? Vince?" once or twice, but the syllables were blown back by the roar of the waters. I said, "Don't waste your breath." We'd have to go down.

Sherry and I stuffed flashlights and other bits of apparatus into our backpacks, handing things back and forth by sheer touch in the darkness. Tilden stood there with his hands at his sides. I assumed he'd gotten his backpack together beforehand, and was watching us fumble. I didn't know what the other two were thinking, but I was thinking we had not brought enough rope, and the climb down—and up again, God willing—would have to be hand-over-hand, like monkeys on a wall. We had enough rope to truss something up and drag it back with us. Plenty for that.

I felt I should try to lighten the mood a little. I put a flashlight under my chin, turned it on fast, made a face at Tilden and growled like a monster. The effect was not what I anticipated. He yelped and cowered. When he took his face away from his hands I saw that he was crying. We had known each other most of our lives, and I never knew Tilden was afraid of the dark.

"Til, man, I'm sorry, I didn't mean to—"

"No . . . it's not you. It's . . ."

He was crying pretty hard now. Shaking. I had no idea what to say to him. I said, "We'll find him, man; he'll be OK."

It was hard to get oriented after that. Tilden was my strength. I wished I had not articulated the phrase "afraid of the dark," for now I was too. This dark was very dark. Tartarus. Deep roaring hell. The flashes of fire and the weird reflections just made it worse. Sherry peered fiercely into the gorge, following the beam of her lamp, so I couldn't see if she was afraid or not.

I lowered the flashlight to the tangle of dampening gear on the damp grass. Worms crisscrossed the ground like tossed red thread, squirming a little in the flashlight beam.

"You stay here," I bellowed. "Man the flashlights. Show us the way as far down as you can."

Tilden nodded, relieved to have something to do.

Actual rain had nearly stopped. The wind kept strong, tearing away at the clouds, and every so often enough the ascending moon appeared that we could climb by it. Moonlight was better than flashlights, for it allowed us use of both hands, and didn't leave a pool of blackness on all sides where the beams didn't reach. Tilden stood topside and aimed the mini-sun of the big Coleman lantern at places where we needed him to. He kept aiming the lantern out and turning in a circle, as if he expected something to come at us from the darkness. Soon the path would bend and the light wouldn't, and Tilden wouldn't be able to hear us over the thunder of the Falls anyway. In daylight you didn't realize how terrible the Falls is, a presence, a thundering, hulking wall beyond which looms utter night. Sane people would not have gone down like that, without sufficient ropes, without a plan, without sure knowledge that what they sought lay at the bottom. I almost didn't, but for the sight of the top of Sherry's head disappearing over the ridge of dark stone, descending into nothing. I followed her.

I knew the ways down pretty well. Sherry knew them better than I expected. Glen was the one who knew them, though. If he had been trying to get away from us, we would never find him. Every time my leg brushed a fern or my arms grazed a dangling blossom, I knew Glen had keyed it out and recorded its name in his diary. Maybe that's what he was doing. Maybe he got distracted by a bug or a liverwort or something and he—

A voice screamed, "Arden?"

"Yeah?"

"You all right?"

It was Tilden's voice from above, sounding a thousand miles away.

"We're fine."

"I couldn't see your light."

"Better to climb by the moon."

"What?"

"Moon. We don't need them. Don't need the lights."

Sherry stood a little lower than I, on a flat-ish space. She held her right hand over her eyes against the Coleman lantern, peering into the black of the gorge for signs of Vince. Unless he was on fire she couldn't have seen him. Her hair was short now, only a little longer than Tilden's and mine. With her breasts concealed under one of my flannel shirts, and that under her slicker, she could be taken for a boy. She was bold as a boy, anyway, swinging herself from rock to rock while I edged down gingerly, wondering sometimes why it all couldn't wait till morning. I caught up to her and we climbed side to side, down the wall slick with rain, but sturdy and rooty and broken enough for there to be more handholds than one might have feared.

We slid under a ridge that cut us off from the glare of the Coleman. There for a moment reigned absolute black. Tilden's voice shouted from above, but it was impossible to hear what he said. Did he drop the lantern? Did he find something? Sherry and I were paralyzed, not knowing which way to move to keep from plunging over the remainder of the cliff into the full body of the flood. Sherry pulled her flashlight out of her pocket and shone it toward the center of the noise. It caught the moving body of the falls, about thirty feet off. The cold wet that beat against us was not rain, but spray from the fierce brown column of turbulent water. She moved the light up toward the top of the falls. The light grew dimmer as it spread to illuminate a wider swath of, essentially, nothing. As her light mounted, Tilden's Coleman appeared again, whiter and more diffuse than the flashlight, and infinitely welcome. The moon came too, breaking through the ceiling to beam broken silver into the heart of the plunge pool. Surrounded by stone, our ears throbbed with the many-times multiplied noise of the river.

When all three lights—Tilden, Sherry, the moon—seemed to meet into one almost sufficient illumination, something appeared at the lip of the pool high above. It was a huge tree, a log mostly, but with a few limbs still attached. It jerked forward, then hesitated. When it stalled in the river, the back-up water flowed over it, submerging it invisible for a moment. Then it rode high on the water again, edging forward. Sherry was pushing hard, backwards against my chest. She screamed at the top of her lungs, "This time it's going to go!"

I didn't know why she was so excited about that until I realized that the log would hurl like a spear into the plunge pool, and like a torpedo across it, and if it followed the course it looked like it must, it would come crashing into our little hollow of a cave. This is why Tilden had moved the lantern, to have a better look. This is why he shouted; he saw it coming.

I pushed Sherry out of the cave, dragging her by the slicker to a ridge of wet stone which the prevailing current in the plunge pool made an unlikely target. We'd just reached its morsel of shelter when the log broke free. It took a surprising amount of time to pass down the front of the falls into the pool. We had not appreciated how shallow the pool was, for the log struck bottom on one end, and, like an acrobat, threw its other end into the air, the hurl and rebound taking its three or four tons exactly where we feared it would, like a battering ram into the mouth of the cave we had just exited.

Tilden screamed from above. I pulled my flashlight out, finally, and moved it across the falls so he would know we were all right. The log whirled around in the chaos of the water, then headed neatly downstream. We heard it bumping and crashing on its way, until it was lost in vaster bumping and crashing further down the gorge. At the place where the tree hit, our little cave was unrecognizable; Sherry and I would have been a stain on the stone.

We had no time to congratulate ourselves on our escape. We assumed that Vinny would have tried to find the space behind the falls—the swifts had to go somewhere—and that unless he was dead and swept down the river, he was there, and if he went there, we could too. The log, aside from nearly killing us, had shown us that the plunge pool, if it was deep at all, was not deep everywhere. We could find a way through it, perhaps even a way around it if the rebounding spray would allow us to search the gorge walls. We'd climbed down as far as we could. We climbed to the Falls as near as we could without being smashed and drowned. The spray pounded a constant shower in our faces, cold, sometimes stinging with debris.

Sherry turned and screamed into my ear, "Maybe he hitched a ride."

"What?"

"On the log! The log! Like in the cartoons. Maybe he—oh, never mind."

We saw where the little shelf of rock ended and where you had to enter the pool or go home. The stone was broken, and perhaps fifty feet of water separated the jagged edge of it from the plunging face of the falls. The bit of pool there had a little shelter from the fallen stones, so the water was not hitting the wall with the velocity it did elsewhere. It was our best bet.

I reached the jagged jumping-off place first. We'd looked carefully enough to know there was no way farther down other than the six foot jump into the pool. I might have done it merrily in daylight, but not then. Here dwelt utter night. No one ever came at night. Nobody sane. If they did, I didn't want to know them. If they did, they likely never came back. I had trouble getting my breath. What might lie in the inky waters? Strange crystals that stabbed, strange rocks that closed over your head . . . Scavengers with bright eyes waiting for fools and suicides to tumble from the cliffs . . . Glen's door, maybe, but a door that didn't lead where he thought it did, but rather into some place horrible and forlorn . . . I don't know that I could have gone a step farther even had I heard Vinny down there crying for help. I'm glad I didn't mock Tilden, for I was paralyzed myself, ninety feet farther down the cliff than him, but still a long way from the bottom.

Sherry screamed, "You ready?"

"He's not down here."

"I think we should see. We're so close."

There was silence. Sherry read my thoughts. I knew she understood when I heard her murmur, "Oh," under her breath. She knew I was terrified. I could go no further. Will was not a factor. Love was not a factor. I could not.

I assumed that was the end of our rescue operation, but Sherry pushed past me and said, "I'm going to try it, then. Will you hold the light on me?"

"Sherry, I don't think—"

Tilden shouted something from the sky. That distracted me, so the next thing I heard was a splash under the myriad splashing, and Sherry crying, "Oh!" as she hit the cold water.

"Sherry!"

"It's so fucking COLD! Where's that light?"

I fumbled around and got the flashlight aimed over the rim of the plunge pool. I trembled with panic. I felt vomit rising in my throat. But when the beam hit the water, making a patch of turbulent brown in the midst of black, I was all right. Sherry was visible and standing. It was only so deep. It was not a hole at the bottom of the world. Panic drained out of me. All I needed was to know what lay beneath. All I needed to know was the farthest one could fall. Sherry was still screeching about the cold while I swept the surface of the pool, trying to find her a way closer to the falls. Her yellow slicker lit up like flame. The water wasn't deep, but the drop to it was high as a man, and Sherry was soaked all over.

"You OK?"

"Except for dripping wet, yes. It was farther than I thought. A little dizzy."

"You jumped without knowing how far it was?"

I could see the shoulders of the slicker shrug.

Something loomed out of the darkness and hit the plunge pool with surprisingly little splash. It had said *fwooosh* all through the air until it said *FAAAAASH* at the surface of the pool. A limb tossed over the falls by the flood waters eddied for a moment, as if deciding which way to go, then headed downstream, gathering speed as it neared the next set of swollen rapids. We had forgotten that, on top of everything else, we should expect a hail of debris from above. Sherry moved away from the center of the pool. She might be safe.

I said, "Hold on." She had jumped and not died. I would too. Before I could think more about it, I launched off the ledge, trying to get as close to Sherry as possible, in case she had hit the one spot without a drop-off.

"You're right. It's fucking cold—"

"What?"

"COLD!"

Sherry laughed a little tinkling laugh. She swept her arm through the air and said, "*Fwoosh,*" in imitation of the debris hailing from the brink of the Falls. Triumphantly I'd kept my light above the water, and she said, "Aim it this way. I can see a hole."

"What?"

"I can see a hole at the side of the Falls. A seam. At the bottom. Must be where the birds go in at night."

The seam presented as a deeper black inside the black. I aimed the flashlight. The beam burned strong on Sherry, but diminished with distance so that the Falls itself was a dim glimmer of black pearl almost outside the range of light. I began to move toward her, feeling the bottom with my boots for crevasses and monsters. The moon had climbed so that the top of the Falls was aflame with silver. It seemed curious to me that none of that pale fire flowed down the Falls to the bottom, it all seemed so liquid, the water and the moonlight, all so much one intermingling substance.

The water came a little above our waists, but was so turbulent with the storm that wavelets climbed almost to our shoulders sometimes. I never imagined there could be so much unevenness in water, so many lumps. In physics class they say that water tends to the level, but they must be talking about some other water. The pool grew shallower as we neared the bottom of the Falls, probably with shelves of shale broken from the cliff. Every time Sherry slipped on a loose stone she yelped a little yelp. Every time she yelped a yelp, I jumped a foot into the air, sure she'd been seized by something terrible. Once she slipped under the surface, came up spluttering and waving her hands in front of her face as though the water were a buzzing insect. I think this is the way heroes really are, yelping and bitching about the cold, but moving intrepidly toward the dark slit in the dark wall while the rest of us look on.

She waited for me to catch up. We had crossed the pool, and stood at the stony rise leading to the floor of the cave behind the Falls. She began to climb, hand over hand, toward a crumbly ledge visible beyond the door. She reached it. She tried it. It did not crumble. She pulled herself out of the water. The floor looked dry behind the falls. Of course it would be—where would the swifts go if everything were filled with water? I followed her exactly, gingerly up the wet stones. I didn't know whether she was going to take the next step into the darkness or not.

Sherry waited until she had my attention. She put her flashlight to her face and made a monster face. Then she plunged behind the Falls.

Momentarily I saw her light behind the falls, dim golden and very beautiful, like a dark curtain shaken in a palace. I took a deep breath and followed.

Beyond the water gate lay blackness. Ravens eating licorice in a coal mine black. Pitch black, without a glimmer, roaring, terrible. I squeezed against the rock wall to get all the way in. It was not necessary to squeeze, for the gap was quite big enough once you were on it. Two could have gone in holding hands. But I wanted to keep my hand on the wall. I wanted something solid at the opposite side of all that resounding, horrible black. It was nothingness made into a world. I had never been more afraid. I figured if I pissed myself it would be OK, as I'd have to swim through the plunge pool to get out again.

"Sherry?" I shouted tentatively into the abyss. She made no answer. She couldn't have heard me anyway in the roar, nor I her. It was like being inside an ear. I moved my hand along the wall. It was not damp. This was surprising. My hand began to hit the bodies of sleeping birds, so I lifted it off the wall and dragged it more lightly along. Feeling the warm backs of the sleeping swifts was better than feeling stone, though also much weirder. I wondered if they felt me, if maybe I entered their sleep as a spirit moving the dark. A few of them stirred or cheeped a little, but mostly I was as impalpable as a dream.

A sensation of openness and fresher air told me I had entered a larger space. I whirled the flashlight around, and though I could see the near wall—indistinct and fuzzy and gently pulsating with the bodies of a million birds—I could not see a roof or a far wall. I did see . . . something . . . I steadied my hand for a systematic investigation, moving tentatively forward in whispering abyss. A rivulet crossed the floor. I doubted it was part of the Falls, but rather a spring welling up from deep inside the cavern. It must flood from time to time, for the space on either side was clear of bird droppings and the bare gray stone shone through, glittering with mica as if with diamond. Beside the rivulet, on a little rise where an exhausted or dying person could lean over and get a drink of water, lay a skeleton. I jumped back, gasping. I dropped the flashlight, then grabbed it before it rolled too close to the bones. I allowed myself to think for one split second what I would have felt had the light gone out.

Over the skeleton, Vinny bent with his face in his hands. His body rocked back and forth. He was so black with muck from the descent only the rocking made you sure he was separate from the black floor of the cave. He rocked back and forth on his knees. You knew he was howling, though the Falls put all of that away.

Raising the flashlight again, I saw Sherry standing behind Vince, her hand on his back, moving with him as he rocked. Behind her the edge of a wall could be discerned, sharp and birdless. Maybe Vinny had scared the birds from that part of the wall.

I shouted to her, "Is he all right?"

She couldn't hear me. She shrugged and then pointed frantically. I whirled around to see the creeping monster she pointed at, but there was nothing. I realized she was pointing at my flashlight. I looked at her carefully. Her mouth said, "Don't lose the light!"

I crossed the cavern and gathered her in my arms. Somehow Sherry had lost her light and mine was the only illumination in the cave. She must have found Vince by touch, or he had found her when briefly the curtain of the dark wavered at the entrance. She seemed tired, or inert. I pulled her toward the door in the water. Finding the way in that direction was easy because of the cool wind sucking forever and forever from the cave into the air. If you were one of the swifts, all you'd have to do is drop down and let the wind carry you. Sherry was a hard pull because she herself was pulling Vince. He would not yet be budged. He kept turning back to the bones and howling, "I WILL NOT LEAVE YOU THIS TIME," audible over all the waters of the world.

I couldn't find a place to stand where I couldn't see the bones. I was afraid of them. I thought they would keep us from ever leaving the cave. Then Sherry lurched forward. She'd finally yanked Vince free. I aimed the flashlight so the bones would see it one last time and know we would return for them.

I didn't remember being so strong. Vince and Sherry both were hanging off me as though they were hurt, me praying to God that they weren't. I dragged them. It was so dark in the cave that night itself seemed a blue blaze, and I dragged them toward that. Stone and wet unfolded into open air.

In the middle of a drama, you forget that things keep happening elsewhere. When the lights went out in the gorge, Tilden feared the worst. He shouted to us for a while, then turned and resolved to run back to the parking lot, hoping that my mother was still there.

None of us understood the immensity of Tilden's fear of the dark. None of us had known about it at all, for when we were with him in the dark, we were with him, and company helped him get through it. He slept with a nightlight, but habit might be blamed as well as fear. During hikes to the Falls, it was he who usually urged an early return, arguing we should get home before the sun had set, but he was always the one with odd jobs and practice, and we assumed he was guarding his sleep. Alone on the ridge of the gorge, with just the Coleman lantern for protection, he was petrified. The shame of not being able to help us in the descent added to his misery, for if there was one thing worse than simple darkness to his heart, it was darkness added to height, the sheer drop into nothingness, the haunted air on all sides and only a few fingers and a few toes tying one to life.

But if he took the lantern we would have no orientation. We would not know where we were, climbing out of the gorge. Our lights had disappeared—he didn't know why—and perhaps for us the Coleman was the only illumination in the world. Tilden swiveled his body in every direction to see what shade or monster might be approaching out of the blackness. He set the lantern on an outcrop of stone where its light would penetrate deepest into the abyss. Then he turned and ran. For a few strides the light of the lantern was with him, blazing the grass around him with the diamonds of after-rain. But then the bend, and utter darkness.

Tilden noticed two things at the moment of utter panic. First, that the low, fat chunk of moon still eked out enough pallor that if anything really formidable were hulking toward him through the trees, he could see it. The second was that the night came on fragrant and soft and beautiful, watery silver where the moon lay upon it, velvet and plush where it did not. A rabbit scurried ahead of him on the path. It was clearly panicked, too, so much so that it never thought to dart to the right or the left, but kept on like an arrow, stupid and stunned. Tilden ran so fast that the rabbit, thinking it was the object of the man's speed, stopped in the path and gave up. It hunkered down, waiting for the fangs at its neck. Tilden leapt over the rabbit and kept running. As he ran he thought of the rabbit, how it had imagined something that was not, how it mistook another drama for its own, how it was never in danger, but crouched panting in the mud, recovering slowly from imagining it was. Tilden recognized himself. Everything that moved in the night moved for its own purpose, and none of it, likely, because of him. The things of the night heard him coming, and were afraid. He too was a dark shape passing in swiftness and power through the thick air. By the time he leapt like a stag over the chain fence around the parking lot, Tilden had become a creature of the night.

Mom still parked there, motor running, lights on—if pointing the wrong way—gospel music coming out of the radio as a fence against the great and terrible night. In one blast of speech, Tilden told as much as was tell-able. Mom whirled back down 414 toward town, to get help. Tilden raced back to the gorge. As he ran, he rejoiced in the darkness. It was not, perhaps the time to do such a thing, but it couldn't be helped. He threw back his head and laughed out loud. The Coleman was like a star beaming on the edge of the precipice. As Tilden ran toward it, the first pale blue seeped into the mountains at his back, the first tentative footfall of dawn.

There was no good place to rest on the ledge under the Falls. Debris fell with the falling water. We danced to one side and then the other, hoping the Falls' aim would be off this one night. I dragged Sherry as hard as I could, and she dragged the shape we had brought with us out of the cave. Back down in the water we went, into the roiling plunge pool. It seemed almost warm now, we had been out in the cold so long. The shape Sherry was dragging made a sound— *oof!*—when it hit the water. He was alive. I whirled with my flashlight and aimed the beam at its face.

"Vinny!"

"Of course 'Vinny,' you retard," Sherry shouted over the waters.

I stalled us in the dangerous pool, looking at Vinny as though I'd never seen him before. It was ludicrous just standing there waiting for someone's chicken coop to fall on our heads.

Vince said, "I went back for him."

I responded, like a dumbass, "Oh."

Suddenly, Vinny took the lead. He moved around us in the pool, still holding Sherry's hand, so I was at the back. I'd been in favor of just lounging around until the firemen came for us, but Vinny hauled heavily out of the pool, tugging Sherry, she tugging me, up the first shelf of the stone tower.

The burst of decisiveness wore Vinny out. He was weak and tired—you could tell that by the way he stumbled—but he still knew the rock wall better than we did. I moved around Sherry to brace Vinny from behind, to catch him if he fell. Sherry held on to my belt, pushing impatiently if Vinny paused too long, considering the way. Dawn hit the rim of the gorge. It was not that far away, not so far as storm and darkness and fear would make one think. The sun shone so beautiful up there, the rain-pearled ferns become a shivery band of emerald.

Welcome hands pulled us out. The firemen arrived—Andy having pulled them from the duties Dadlez gave them farther up the river—and jumped down to help us the rest of the way. One tried to carry Sherry. I heard her say, about ten feet behind me, "I can manage on my own, thank you very much. Just give me your hand. That's all I need."

First thing I saw as we clawed our way over the rim was Chief Dadlez pulling up in his muddy cruiser. He and Officer Big City got out of the cruiser, surveyed the scene, and put their fists on their hips with exactly the same motion at exactly the same time.

"Is somebody going to catch me up?" Dadlez barked, as though everything had gone awry in his absence.

My dad, bless his heart, said, "Found 'em."

Vinny had not spoken all the way up from the pool. I heard Lucas Mills the volunteer fireman, and my cousin in some complicated way—ask how he was, and Vinny had not answered. Behind my dad, Coach was bent over with his hands on his knees, like he'd been throwing up. Dad had his hand on his back, comforting him. He stood up, Coach did, and began to walk toward his son. Not many people heard what he said, or even knew that he'd said anything.

But I did. He said, "You find what you were looking for?"

Vince nodded.

I lost track of how long they stood there, looking at one another, but at last Coach said, "Son," and pulled Vince against him so Vince's face was buried in his shoulder. Vince sagged at the knees and his father held him up. The rain stopped finally, even way out over the green mountains. The men went down for the bones, then, Andy and Lucas and the firemen did, with a stretcher like the bones were still a man. I could see Vince walking a little ahead when the dawn broke, with his dad's arm across his shoulders. The pack was on his back, the one with the Boy Scout patches, catching the first light sapphire and gold. Vince would abide there and wait for the bones, to be with them in the next part of their journey. We would wait with him until the next thing happened.

BIOGRAPHICAL NOTE

David Brendan Hopes, whose novel *The Falls of the Wyona* was chosen for Red Hen Press's 2017 Quill Prize, is a poet, playwright, and painter living in Asheville, North Carolina. Originally from Ohio, Hopes taught at Hiram College, Syracuse University, Phillips Exeter Academy, and is now Professor of English at UNCA. His prize-winning plays have been produced in New York, Chicago, Los Angeles, Cincinnati, Seattle, and London, and his publications have been in venues as diverse as *Audubon*, the *New Yorker*, and *Best American Poetry, 2016*.

Previous full-length publications include *The Glacier's Daughters* (Juniper Prize, UMass Press), *Blood Rose* (Urthona Press), *A Dream of Adonis* (Pecan Grove Press), and *Peniel* (Saint Julian Press). Nonfiction publications include: *A Sense of the Morning* (Milkweed Editions), *Bird Songs of the Mesozoic* (Milkweed Editions), and *A Childhood in the Milky Way* (Akron University Press). He has twice received the North Carolina New Play Project Prize, as well as the Holland New Voices Playwriting Award, the Sprenger Foundation Award for Historical Drama, the Desert Star Award for Best Original Writing, the Arch and Bruce Brown Foundation Award for Playwriting, and the Siena Playwrights' Prize. Previously in fiction, he has won the William Van Dyke Short Story Prize, the E.M. Koeppel Short Fiction Award, the Sonora Review Fiction Prize, and the Hohenburg Award in Fiction. Poetry accolades include the Juniper Prize, the Saxifrage Prize, the Nazim Hikmet Prize, and the Utmost Christian Writers Christian Poetry Award.